Herbert Wilkinson

Legends of Ancient Rome

Herbert Wilkinson

Legends of Ancient Rome

ISBN/EAN: 9783744781190

Printed in Europe, USA, Canada, Australia, Japan

Cover: Foto ©Andreas Hilbeck / pixelio.de

More available books at **www.hansebooks.com**

Elementary Classics.

LEGENDS OF ANCIENT ROME.

FROM LIVY.

ADAPTED AND EDITED, WITH NOTES, EXERCISES, AND
VOCABULARIES,

BY

HERBERT WILKINSON, M.A.,
FORMERLY POSTMASTER OF MERTON COLLEGE, OXFORD

London:
MACMILLAN AND CO.,
AND NEW YORK.
1890.

PREFACE.

THIS selection has been compiled for the use of boys who could make out an easy passage of such an author as Caesar, but would be stopped by long or difficult sentences. It is hoped that the passages will be found, at any rate in the earlier part of the book, to be of progressive difficulty. The attempt to attain this end has led to the omission of some legends of the kings which could not have been made easy enough without much alteration of the text. As this would have left them not Livy's, but something very inferior, it was thought better to omit them altogether.

The text has been simplified mainly by omissions, which have sometimes been large. Moral and political reflections, and many rhetorical passages, have been left out bodily. Elaborate periods have been omitted, or, where they contained matter essential to the story, broken up. In one or two places the order of words has been simplified where it seemed likely to offer needless difficulty to young boys.

v

CONTENTS.

LEGENDS OF ANCIENT ROME.

I. The Founding of Rome.

PROCAE, regi Albae, duo filii Numitor atque Amulius erant. Numitori, qui natu maximus erat, pater regnum vetustum gentis legat. Plus tamen vis potuit[1] quam voluntas patris; pulso fratre Amulius regnat. Addit sceleri scelus; fratris filios interemit, filiam Ream Silviam Vestalem[2] legit. Quae quum filios geminos edidisset, ipsa vincta in custodiam datur, pueros Amulius in fluentem aquam mitti jubet.

Forte quadam Tiberis super ripas effusus erat, nec ad ipsum flumen usquam adiri poterat. Itaque ii qui infantes ferebant, velut defuncti regis imperio, in proxima alluvie pueros exponunt. Vastae tum in his locis solitudines erant. Fama est, quum aqua fluitantem alveum, quo expositi erant pueri, in sicco destituisset, lupam sitientem ex montibus ad pueri-

A

lem vagitum cursum flexisse. Eam mammas infantibus praebentem a magistro regii pecoris inventam esse. Huic Faustulo[3] nomen fuisse ferunt, ab eo Larentiae uxori educandos datos esse.

Ita geniti itaque educati, quum primum adoleverunt venando peragrabant saltus. Hinc robore corporibus animisque sumpto, in latrones praeda onustos impetus faciebant pastoribusque rapta dividebant. Tum latrones, ob iram praedae amissae, Remum ex insidiis ceperunt, captum regi Amulio tradiderunt, dicentes impetus in Numitoris agros a fratribus fieri. Itaque Numitori ad supplicium Remus deditur.

Jam ab initio Faustulo spes fuerat regiam stirpem apud se educari; nam et expositos esse jussu regis infantes sciebat, et tempus, quo ipse eos sustulisset, ad id ipsum[4] congruere; sed rem nisi per necessitatem aperire noluerat. Jam metu subactus Romulo rem aperit. Forte et Numitori,[5] quum in custodia Remum haberet, audivissetque geminos esse fratres, memoria nepotum animum tetigerat, et haud procul erat quin Remum agnosceret. Ita Amulio undique dolus nectitur. Romulus cum pastoribus in regem impetum facit, et a domo Numitoris, alia comparata manu, adjuvat Remus. Ita regem obtruncant. Numitor, postquam juvenes, perpetrata caede, gratulantes ad se pergere vidit, extemplo advocato concilio, scelera fratris, originem nepotum, caedem tyranni ostendit. Quum juvenes, per medium contionem ingressi, **avum regem** salutassent, **vox ex** omni multitudine **consentiens** Numitori **imperium** defert.

Ita re[6] Albana Numitori permissa, Romulum Remumque cepit cupido urbis condendae **in his** locis ubi expositi erant. Ad id magnus Albanorum Latinorumque numerus, pastores quoque accesserant. Sed regni cupidine foedum certamen inter fratres coortum est. Quoniam gemini erant, nec aetate discrimen facere poterant, rem auguriis discernere constituunt. Palatium Romulus Remus Aventinum montem cepit. Priori **Remo** augurium venisse **fertur sex** volucres, jamque nuntiato augurio duplex numerus Romulo sese ostendit. Ita utrumque sua multitudo regem salutat. **Inde** cum altercatione congressi, ad caedem vertuntur. Ibi Remus in turba ictus **cecidit.** Vulgatior fama est Remum ludibrio fratris novos transiluisse muros; inde ab irato Romulo interfectum esse. Ita solus Romulus imperio potitus, condita urbs conditoris nomine appellata est.

II. THE RAPE OF THE SABINE WOMEN.

JAM res Romana adeo valida erat **ut** cuilibet finitimarum civitatum bello par esset, sed penuria erat mulierum, quod Romanis conubia cum finitimis non erant. tum ex consilio patrum Romulus legatos circa **vicinas gentes** misit, **qui** societatem conubiumque novo populo peterent ; nusquam benigne legatio audita est. Romani id aegre passi, ad vim spectabant. Romulus autem, iram dissimulans, ludos solemnes Neptuno parat. Indici inde finitimis spectaculum jubet. Multi mortales studio novae urbis videndae convenerant, et Sabinorum omnis multitudo cum liberis ac conjugibus adfuere. Ubi spectaculi tempus venit et mentes omnium cum oculis huic deditae erant, tum signo dato juventus Romana ad rapiendas virgines discurrit. Turbato per metum ludicro, maesti parentes virginum profugiunt, deum invocantes, cujus ad ludos decepti venissent. Nec raptis indignatio est minor. Sed Romulus ipse circumibat. docebatque superbia patrum id factum esse, qui conubium finitimis negassent ; mollirent modo iras, et iis animos darent quibus fors corpora dedisset. Jam admodum mitigati animi raptis erant ; at raptarum parentes, lacrimis et querelis civitates concitabant, bellumque a Sabinis ortum est. Conserto proelio Sabinae mulieres, quarum ex injuria bellum ortum erat, crinibus passis scissaque veste ausae sunt se inter tela volantia inferre, et infestas acies dirimere, hinc patres, hinc viros orantes ne soceri generique se nefando sanguine respergerent. Movet res quum multitudinem tum duces. Silentium et repentina fit quies ; inde ad foedus faciendum duces prodeunt, nec pacem modo sed civitatem unam ex duabus faciunt, regnum consociant, imperium omne Romam conferunt.

III. The Horatii and the Curiatii.

Tullo Hostilio rege bellum inter Romanos Albanos-que coortum est. Forte in duobus **tum** exercitibus erant trigemini fratres, nec aetate **nec** viribus dis-pares. Horatios Curiatiosque fuisse constat, incertum tamen est utrius populi Horatii, utrius Curiatii fuerint. Plures tamen sunt qui Romanos Horatios vocent. Cum trigeminis **agunt**[1] reges **ut pro sua** quisque patria ferro dimicent : ibi imperium **fore ubi** victoria **fuerit.** Nihil excusatur; tempus et locus convenit. Priusquam **dimicarent** foedus **ictum est inter** Romanos **et** Albanos ut, cujus populi cives eo certamine vicis-sent, is alteri populo cum bona pace imperitaret.

Foedere icto trigemini arma capiunt. Duo exercitus utrimque pro castris consederant. Datur signum, infestisque armis terni juvenes concurrunt. Consertis deinde manibus,[2] duo Romani, vulneratis tribus Albanis, interfecti sunt. Ad quorum casum conclam-avit gaudio **A**lbanus exercitus, Romanas legiones jam spes tota deseruerat. Is tamen qui ex Romanis super-fuit forte integer erat ; **ergo** ut segregaret hostium pugnam, capessit fugam, eos ita secuturos ratus ut quemque vulnera sinerent. Jam aliquantum spatii ex eo loco ubi pugnatum **est** aufugerat, quum respiciens videt magnis intervallis sequentes, unum haud procul ab sese abesse. **In** eum magno impetu rediit ; et **dum** Albanus exercitus inclamat Curiatiis **ut** opem ferant fratri, jam Horatius caeso hoste victor secundam pugnam petebat. Tunc clamore Romani militem suum adjuvant, et ille defungi proelio festinat. Prius itaque quam alter, qui nec procul aberat, consequi posset, et alterum Curiatium conficit. Jamque aequato Marte singuli supererant, sed nec spe nec viribus pares. Alter ferro intactus et geminata victoria ferox in certamen tertium ibat, alter vulnere ac cursu fessus, fratrumque ante se strage victus, hosti victori objicitur. Nec illud proelium fuit. Romanus exultans, "duos," inquit, "fratrum manibus dedi, tertium ut Romanus Albano imperet dabo." Arma male sustinenti gladium jugulo defigit, jacentem spoliat. Romani ovantes ac gratulantes Horatium accipiunt eo³ majore cum gaudio quo prope metum res fuerat. Sepulcra exstant quo quisque loco accidit, duo Romana uno loco propius Albam, tria Albana Romam versus, sed distantia locis ut et pugnatum est.

IV. How Horatius Defended the Bridge.
B.C. 508.

The Romans had driven out their king, L. Tarquinius, with all his family on account of his tyranny. Now the Tarquins were of Etruscan origin, so they sought help of their kinsmen in Etruria.

Jam Tarquinii ad Lartem Porsenam, Clusinum regem, perfugerant, orabantque ne se in exilio vivere pateretur. Porsena igitur Romam infesto exercitu venit. Quum hostes adessent, omnes in urbem ex agris demi-

graverunt, urbem ipsam praesidiis firmaverunt. Pons
Sublicius iter paene hostibus dedit; **sed** unus **vir**
Horatius Cocles, qui forte in statione **pontis** positus
erat, quum Janiculum **repentino impetu** captum vi-
disset, trepidamque suorum turbam arma ordinesqu**e**
relinquere, admonuit ut pontem ferro atque igni **inter-**
rumperent. Promisit se, quantum vir unus **posset,**
hostes sustenturum esse. Vadit inde ad primum **adi-**
tum pontis; duos tamen ex Romanis **pudor** cum eo
tenuit, Sp. Lartium ac T. Herminium. **Cum his** primam periculi procellam parumper sustinuit. **Deinde**
eos quoque ipsos, exigua parte pontis relicta, in **tutum**
cedere coegit. Circumferens inde oculos ad **proceres**
Etruscorum, nunc singulos **provocabat, nunc** omnes
increpabat. Aliquamdiu cunctati **sunt dum** alius
alium circumspectat ut proelium incipiat. Pudor
deinde commovit aciem, et clamore sublato und**ique in**
unum hostem tela conjiciunt. Quae **quum in objecto**
scuto cuncta haesissent, neque minus obstinatus ille
pontem obtineret, jam impetu facto virum detrudere
conabantur, quum simul fragor rupti pontis, simul
clamor Romanorum pavore subito impetum sustinuit.
Tum Cocles, "Tiberine pater," inquit, **"te** precor ut
haec arma et hunc militem propitio flumine accipias."
Inde armatus in Tiberim desiluit, multisque superinci-
dentibus telis incolumis ad suos tranavit. Grata
erga tantam virtutem civitas fuit; statua Horatii in
comitio posita, agri quantum **uno die** circumarare
potuit datum est.

V. The Daring of Mucius Scaevola.
B.C. 508.

Urbe ab Horatio servata, obsidio erat nihilominus
et frumenti inopia, sedendoque expugnaturum se urbem
Porsena sperabat, quum C. Mucius, adolescens nobilis,
magno audacique facinore eam indignitatem[1] vindican-
dam esse ratus, sua sponte in hostium castra penetrare
constituit.   Dein, metuens ne, si consulum injussu et
ignaris omnibus[2] iret, forte deprehensus a custodibus
Romanis retraheretur ut transfuga, senatum adit.
"Transire Tiberim," inquit, "patres, et intrare, si
possim, castra hostium volo, non praedo nec populati-
onum ultor; majus, dis juvantibus, in animo est
facinus." Approbant patres. Abdito intra vestem
ferro proficiscitur.   Ubi eo venit, in confertissima
turba prope regium tribunal constitit.   Ibi quum
stipendium militibus forte daretur, et scriba, cum rege
sedens pari fere ornatu, multa ageret, Mucius, timens
sciscitari uter Porsena esset, ne regem ignorando
semet ipse aperiret quis esset, scribam pro rege ob-
truncat.   Inde dum per trepidam turbam cruento
mucrone viam sibi ipse facit, regii satellites comprehensum[3] retraxerunt.   Ante tribunal regis destitutus,
tum quoque inter tantas fortunae minas metuendus
magis quam metuens, "Romanus sum," inquit "civis:
C. Mucium vocant.   Hostis[4] hostem occidere volui.
nec ad mortem minus animi est quam fuit ad

caedem. **Romanum** est et facere et pati. Nec **unus** in te **hos** animos gessi ; juventus tibi Romana omnis bellum indicit. Ne aciem, ne proelium timueris ; **uni** tibi et cum singulis res erit." Tum **rex** simul ira commotus periculoque conterritus, ignem circumdari **jussit** nisi propere exponeret quas sibi insidias minaretur. Mucius autem, ut monstraret se corporis dolorem **nihili facere** dextram accenso ad sacrificium foculo injecit. Rex, tantam fortitudinem miratus, **amoveri** ab altaribus juvenem jussit, et liberum inviolatumque dimisit. Tunc Mucius, " **Beneficio**," inquit, "a me id tulisti **quod** minis nequisti ; trecenti juventutis Romanae principes conjuravimus **ut in te hac via** grassaremur. Mea prima **sors fuit; ceteri suo quisque** tempore **aderunt**." Huic, quum **Romam** rediisset, Scaevolae **a clade** dextrae manus **cognomen datum** est.

VI. THE BATTLE OF LAKE REGILLUS.

B.C. 499.

Porsena having made peace with Rome, Tarquinius went to live in exile at Tusculum in Latium, and joined the Latins in a war with Rome, hoping thus to recover his throne.

Aulus Postumius dictator, Titus Aebutius magister equitum cum magnis copiis peditum equitumque profecti, ad lacum Regillum in agro Tusculano agmini hostium occurrerunt, et quia Tarquinios esse in exercitu Latinorum auditum est, Romani sustineri non potuerunt quin extemplo confligerent. Ergo proelium etiam gravius atque atrocius quam caetera fuit. Duces enim non modo ad regendam consilio rem adfuere, sed suis ipsi corporibus dimicaverunt, nec quisquam ferme procerum hac aut illa ex acie praeter dictatorem Romanum sine vulnere excessit. In Postumium suos adhortantem Tarquinius Superbus, quamquam jam aetate erat gravior, equum admisit, ictusque ab latere, concursu suorum in tutum receptus est. Et ad [1] alterum cornu Aebutius magister equitum in Octavium Mamilium ducem Tusculanum impetum fecit. Hic quoque equum concitat, tantaque vi concursum est [2] ut brachium Aebutio trajectum sit, Mamilio pectus percussum. Hunc quidem in secundam aciem Latini recepere; Aebutius, quum saucio brachio telum tenere non posset, pugna excessit. Dux Latinus vulnere nihil deterritus, proelium renovat, et quia suos metu perculsos videbat, arcessit cohortem exulum Romanorum, cui Luci Tarquini filius praeerat. Hi quod majore pugnabant ira ob erepta bona patriamque ademptam, pugnam parumper restituerunt.

Referentibus jam pedem Romanis, M. Valerius, conspicatus ferocem juvenem Tarquinium ostentantem se in prima exulum acie, subdit calcaria equo, et Tarquinium infesto spiculo petit. Tarquinius retro in agmen suorum cessit. Valerium, temere invectum in exulum aciem, ex transverso quidam adortus transfigit; equo autem vulnere equitis non retardato, moribundus Romanus ad terram defluxit. Dictator Postumius, postquam cecidisse talem virum, exules citato agmine invehi, **suos** perculsos cedere animadvertit, cohorti **suae,** quam praesidii causa circa **se** habebat, dat signum ut quem [3] suorum fugientem viderint, illum **pro** hoste habeant. Romanis ita **a** fuga in hostem versis acies restituta est. Cohors dictatoris tum primum proelium iniit. Integris corporibus animisque fessos exules adorti [4] caedunt. **Ibi** alia pugna inter proceres coorta est. Imperator Latinus, **ubi** cohortem exulum **a** dictatore Romano prope circumventam vidit, quosdam ex **suis in** primam aciem secum rapit. **T.** Herminius, legatus Romanus, Mamilium veste **armisque** noscitans, tanta **vi** cum hostium **duce** proelium iniit ut Mamilium uno **ictu** per latus **trans-fixum** [4] **occiderit**; ipse autem, **dum** corpus hostis spoliat, jaculo transfixus expiraverit. Tum dictator ad equites advolat, obtestans **ut** fesso jam pedite descendant ex equis, **et** pugnam ineant. Dicto paruere; desiliunt **ex** equis, provolant in primum. Recipit extemplo animum pedestris acies, postquam juventutis proceres secum partem periculi sustinentes vidit. Tum demum impulsi Latini, perculsaque inclinavit acies. Equitibus admoti sunt equi, ut persequi hostes possent, secuta est et pedestris acies, tantusque ardor fuit ut Romani eodem impetu quo fuderant hostem, castra caperent. **Hoc** modo ad lacum Regillum pugnatum est. Dictator **et** magister equitum triumphantes in urbem rediere.

VII. The Story of Coriolanus.

B.C. 492-488.

The Volscians were a tribe in Latium who were repeatedly at war with Rome, and were not finally conquered till B.C. 338.

Consul ad Volscum bellum missus oppidum Coriolos magna vi adortus est. Erat tum in castris inter primores juvenum Cn. Marcius, cui cognomen postea Coriolano fuit. Dum exercitus Romanus Coriolos obsidet, sine ullo metu extrinsecus imminentis belli, legiones Volscae ab Antio profectae invadunt. eodemque tempore ex oppido eruperunt hostes. Marcius, qui forte in statione erat, cum delecta militum manu non modo impetum erumpentium retudit, sed per patentem portam irrupit, caedeque facta, aedificiis muro imminentibus ignem injecit. Inde oppidanorum ortus clamor et Romanis auxit animum et Volscos qui ad ferendam opem venerant, utpote capta urbe, turbavit. Ita fusi sunt Volsci, Corioli oppidum captum.

M. Minucio et A. Sempronio consulibus, magna vis frumenti ex Sicilia advecta est, agitatumque in senatu quanti[1] plebi daretur. Multi ex patribus venisse tempus putabant recuperandi jura[2] quae sibi vi extorta essent. In primis Marcius Coriolanus, hostis tribuniciae potestatis, " si annonam," inquit, " veterem volunt, jus pristinum reddant patribus." Et senatui nimis atrox haec sententia visa est, et plebem ira prope armavit. Tribuni diem Marcio dixerunt,[3] qui quum die dicta non adesset, damnatus absens in

Volscos exulatum abiit. Venientem Volsci benigne exceperunt, benigniusque indies colebant. Hospitio utebatur Atti Tulli, qui longe princeps Volsci nominis erat, Romanisque semper infestus. Itaque quum alterum vetus odium, alterum ira recens stimularet, consilia de Romano bello conferunt.

Imperatores ad id bellum a Volscis lecti Attius Tullius et Cn. Marcius, exul Romanus. Hic Circeios profectus, primum colonos inde Romanos expulit liberamque eam urbem Volscis tradidit. Inde in Latinam viam transgressus, multa oppida Romanis ademit. Postremo castris quinque millia ab urbe positis agrum Romanum populatur, custodibus inter populatores missis qui patriciorum agros intactos servarent, sive plebi infensus, sive ut discordia inde inter patres plebemque oreretur. Quae profecto orta esset, sed externus timor, maximum concordiae vinculum, infensos inter se jungebat animos.

Sp. Nautius et Sex. Furius consules erant. Eos, dum legiones recensent et praesidia per muros disponunt, multitudo ingens vocare senatum, referre[4] de legatis ad Cn. Marcium mittendis coegit. Missi itaque de pace ad Marcium oratores. Atrox responsum retulerunt; si Volscis ager redderetur, posse agi de pace; si praeda belli per otium frui vellent, se enisurum ut appareret non fractum exilio sibi animum esse. Sacerdotes quoque ivisse supplices ad castra hostium traditum est, nec magis quam legatos Marci animum flexisse.

Tum matronae ad Veturiam, matrem Coriolani, Volumniamque uxorem frequentes coeunt. Pervicere ut et Veturia, magno natu mulier, et Volumnia duos parvos filios secum ferens in castra hostium irent, et quoniam armis viri defendere urbem non possent, mulieres precibus lacrimisque defenderent. Ubi ad castra ventum est, nuntiatumque Coriolano est adesse ingens mulierum agmen, primo, qui neque a legatis neque a sacerdotibus motus esset, multo obstinatior adversus lacrimas muliebres erat. Deinde familiarium quidam, qui Veturiam inter ceteras cognoverat inter nurum nepotesque stantem, "Nisi me frustrantur," inquit, "oculi, mater tibi conjuxque et liberi adsunt." Coriolanus quum matri complexum ferret, mulier in iram ex precibus versa, "Sine, priusquam complexum accipio," inquit, "sciam utrum ad filium an ad hostem venerim, captiva materne in castris tuis sim." Uxor deinde ac liberi amplexi, fletusque ab omni turba ortus virum tandem fregere. Complexus inde suos dimittit ; ipse retro ab urbe castra movit. Abductis deinde legionibus ex agro Romano, alii alio⁵ leto periisse eum tradunt.

VIII. The War of the Fabii with the People of Veii. b.c. 479, 478.

Veii was one of the most powerful cities of Etruria. In Nos. XI. and XII. its final conquest by Rome will be related.

Eo tempore neque pax neque bellum cum Veientibus fuit. Res in latrocinium venerat ; legionibus Romanis cedebant in urbem : ubi abductas senserant legiones, agros incursabant. Ita neque omitti res neque perfici poterat.

Tum Fabia gens senatum adit ; consul pro gente loquitur :—"Assiduo magis quam magno praesidio, ut scitis, patres conscripti,[1] bellum Veiens eget. Vos alia bella curate, Fabios hostes Veientibus date. Sic tuta majestas Romani nominis erit. Id velut familiare bellum privato sumptu gerere nobis in animo est." Gratiae ingentes actae. Consul e curia egressus comitante Fabiorum agmine, qui in vestibulo curiae senatus consultum expectantes steterant, domum rediit. Jussi armati postero die ad limen consulis adesse. Domos inde discedunt.

Fabii postero die arma capiunt ; quo jussi erant conveniunt. Consul paludatus egrediens in vestibulo gentem omnem suam instructo agmine videt ; acceptus in medium signa ferri jubet. Nunquam exercitus neque minor numero neque clarior fama et admiratione hominum per urbem incessit. Sex et trecenti milites, quorum neminem ducem sperneres, ibant, unius familiae viribus Veienti populo pestem minitantes. Quibus Capitolium arcemque et alia templa praetereuntibus, magna sequentium turba deos precatur ut illud agmen faustum atque felix mittant, sospites brevi in patriam ad parentes restituant. Incassum missae preces. Infelici via, dextro Jano[2] portae Carmentalis profecti, ad Cremeram flumen perveniunt. Is opportunus locus communiendo praesidio visus est.

L. Aemilius inde et C. Servilius consules facti. Et donec in populationibus res erat, non ad praesidium modo tutandum Fabii satis erant, sed tota regione qua Tuscus ager Romano adjacet, sua tuta omnia, infesta[3] hostium fecere. Intervallum deinde haud magnum populationibus fuit, dum et Veientes, accito ex Etruria exercitu, praesidium Cremerae oppugnant, et Romanae legiones, ab L. Aemilio consule adductae, cominus cum Etruscis acie dimicant. Veientibus vix spatium fuit aciem dirigendi ; ita fusi ad Saxa Rubra —ibi castra habebant—pacem supplices petunt, cujus impetratae mox eos paenituit. Rursus cum Fabiis erat Veienti[1] populo certamen. Nec erant incursiones modo in agros, aut subiti impetus in incursantes, sed aliquotiens aequo campo collatisque signis[4] certatum est ; gensque una populi Romani saepe ex opulentissima Etrusca civitate victoriam tulit. Id primo acerbum indignumque Veientibus est visum ; inde consilium natum est insidiis ferocem hostem captandi. Gaudebant etiam multo successu Fabiis audaciam crescere. Itaque et pecora praedantibus aliquotiens obviam acta sunt, velut casu incidissent, et agrestium fuga vasti relicti sunt agri, et subsidia armatorum, ad arcendas populationes missa, saepius simulato quam vero pavore refugerunt. Jamque Fabii adeo contempserant hostem ut sua arma neque loco neque tempore ullo sustineri posse crederent. Haec spes eos provexit ut ad pecora procul a Cremera conspecta decurrerent, quamquam rara hostium arma apparebant. **Quum** improvidi effuso cursu insidias circa ipsum **iter** locatas superassent, et vaga pecora raperent, subito ex insidiis **undique** consurgunt hostes. Fabii, clamore exterriti, et jam agmine armatorum saepti, cogebantur in spatium brevissimum se **colligere**; quae res et paucitatem **eorum et** multitudinem Etruscorum insignem faciebat. Tum omissa pugna, quam in omnes partes **intenderant, in unum** locum se omnes inclinant. Eo nisi corporibus **armisque rupere viam. Duxit** via in editum leniter collem. **Inde primo restitere;** mox, **ut** respirandi **spatium superior** locus dedit, pepulere etiam subeuntes, vicissetque auxilio loci paucitas, **nisi** jugo circummissi Veientes in verticem **collis** evasissent. **Ita superior** rursus factus hostis. Fabii caesi ad **unum omnes,** praesidiumque expugnatum. Trecentos sex periisse constat, unum prope puberem relictum, stirpem genti Fabiae, dubiisque **rebus** populi Romani maximum futurum auxilium.[5]

IX. THE STORY OF CINCINNATUS.

B.C. 458.

*The Aequi were **a** tribe living on the eastern boundary of Latium, and like the **Volsci** constantly at **war with** Rome.*

CONSUL MINUCIUS, **quum in** fines Aequorum **exercitum** duxisset, nulla **clade** accepta in castris se pavidus tenebat. Quod ubi senserunt hostes, crevit ex metu alieno, **ut** fit, audacia; **et** nocte adorti castra, postquam vis aperta parum profecerat, munitiones postero die circumdant. Quae priusquam omnem clauderent exitum, quinque equites, inter stationes hostium emissi, Romam pertulere consulem exercitumque obsideri. Nihil tam inopinatum nec tam insperatum accidere potuit. Itaque tantus pavor, tanta trepidatio fuit, quanta, si urbem, non castra, hostes obsiderent. Quum dictatorem dici placuisset[1] qui rem perculsam restitueret, L. Quinctius Cincinnatus consensu omnium dicitur.

L. Quinctius, spes unica imperii populi Romani, trans Tiberim agrum quatuor jugerum colebat, quae prata Quinctia vocantur. Ibi, operi agresti intentus, ab legatis rogatus ut mandata senatus togatus audiret, togam e tugurio proferre uxorem jubet. Qua velatus simulac pulvere et sudore absterso processit, dictatorem cum legati gratulantes salutant; in urbem vocant; qui terror sit in exercitu exponunt. Navis Quinctio publice parata fuit, transvectumque tres filii, obviam egressi, excipiunt, inde alii propinqui atque amici, tum patrum major pars. Antecedentibus lictoribus domum deductus est; et illa quidem nocte vigilatum est in urbe.

Postero die dictator, quum ante lucem in forum venisset, magistrum equitum dicit L. Tarquitium patriciae gentis, qui bello longe primus Romanae juventutis habitus est. Cum magistro equitum in contionem venit, justitium edicit, claudi tabernas tota urbe jubet, vetat quemquam privatae quidquam rei agere. Tum imperavit omnibus qui aetate militari[2] essent ut armati cum cibariis in dies quinque coctis, vallisque duodenis ante solis occasum Martis in Campo adessent. Ceteros quibus aetas ad militandum gravior esset militibus cibaria coquere jussit. Sic juventus ad vallos petendos discurrit. Sumpsere unde[3] cuique proximum fuit ; prohibitus nemo est, impigreque ad edictum dictatoris praesto fuere. Inde composito agmine legiones ipse dictator, magister equitum suos equites ducit. Media nocte in Algidum perveniunt, et ut sensere se jam prope hostes esse, signa constituunt.

Ibi dictator, equo circumvectus, formamque castrorum, quantum nocte prospici poterat, contemplatus, tribunis militum imperavit ut sarcinas in unum conjici juberent, militem cum armis vallisque in ordines suos redire. Facta sunt quae imperavit. Tum exercitum omnem longo agmine circumdat hostium castris, et, ubi signum datum sit, clamorem omnes tollere jubet, clamore sublato ante se quemque ducere fossam, et jacere vallum. Jussa miles exsequitur ; clamor hostes circumsonat ; superat inde castra hostium et in castra consulis venit : alibi[4] pavorem, alibi gaudium ingens facit. Consul, civium esse clamorem atque auxilium adesse ratus, suos arma capere et se subsequi jubet. Nocte proelium initum est. Aequi, ab exteriore ad interiorem hostem versi, dictatori noctem ad opus perficiendum dedere ; pugnatumque cum consule ad

lucem est. Prima luce jam circumvallati ab dictatore
erant, et vix adversus unum exercitum pugnam
sustinebant. Tum hostes, ancipiti malo urgente
a proelio ad preces versi, hinc dictatorem, hinc
consulem orare,[5] ne in occidione victoriam ponerent,
ut inermes se inde abire sinerent. Dictator Grac-
chum Cloelium ducem principesque alios vinctos ad
se adduci jubet. Negat se sanguinis Aequorum
egere; licere abire; sed ut exprimatur tandem confessio subactam domitamque esse gentem, sub
jugum[6] abituros. Tribus hastis jugum fit, duabus
humi fixis, superque eas una transversa deligata.
Sub hoc jugo dictator Aequos misit.

Castris hostium receptis plenis omnium rerum—
nudos enim emiserat—praedam omnem suo tantum
militi dedit; consularem exercitum ipsumque consulem increpans; "Carebis," inquit, "praedae parte,
miles, ex eo hoste cui prope praedae[7] fuisti: et
tu, L. Minuci, donec consularem animum incipias
habere, legatus his legionibus praeeris." Ita se
Minucius abdicat consulatu, jussusque ad exercitum
manet. Romae senatus a Q. Fabio, praefecto urbis,
habitus[8] triumphantem Quinctium urbem ingredi
jussit. Ducti ante currum hostium duces, militaria
signa praelata, secutus exercitus praeda onustus.
Epulae instructae esse dicuntur ante omnium domos,
epulantesque cum carmine triumphali currum secuti
sunt. Quinctius sexto decimo die dictatura in sex
menses accepta se abdicavit.

X. How Cossus Won the Spolia Opima.

B.C. 437.

Hoc anno Fidenae, colonia Romana, ad Lartem Tolum-
nium Veientium regem defecere. Majus additum est
defectioni **scelus** ; legatos Romanos, **causam novi con-**
silii quaerentes, **jussu Tolumnii interfecerunt.** Cum
Veientibus Fidenatibusque atrox **dimicatio instabat.**
Consules **creantur M.** Geganius Macerinus tertium,[1]
et L. **Sergius Fidenas ; quem credo a bello quod**
deinde **gessit** appellatum esse. Hic enim primus cis
Anienem flumen cum rege **Veientium** secundo proelio
conflixit **nec** incruentam **victoriam retulit.** Major
itaque **ex civibus amissis dolor** quam laetitia fusis
hostibus **fuit ; et senatus,** ut in trepidis **rebus,** dictatorem dici Mamercum Aemilium jussit. Is magistrum
equitum **L.** Quinctium Cincinnatum, dignum parente
juvenem dixit. **Ad** delectum a consulibus habitum
centuriones veteres belli periti adjecti sunt, et numerus
amissorum proxima pugna expletus. Dictator inde
hostes ex agro Romano trans Anienem submovit,
collesque inter Fidenas atque Anienem cepit, nec ante
in campos degressus est quam legiones Faliscorum
auxilio venerunt. **Tum** demum castra Etruscorum
pro moenibus Fidenarum posita sunt ; et dictator
haud **procul inde ad** confluentes consedit, vallo in
ripis utriusque amnis interposito. Postero die suos
in aciem eduxit.

Inter hostes variae fuere sententiae. Faliscus[2] procul ab domo militiam aegre patiens, satisque sibi fidens, pugnam poscere :[3] Veienti Fidenatique plus spei in trahendo bello esse. Tolumnius, quamquam suorum magis placebant consilia, postero tamen die se pugnaturum edixit ne longinquam militiam non paterentur Falisci. Dictatori et Romanis, quod detrectasset pugnam hostis, animi accessere; posteroque die acies utrimque inter bina[4] castra in medium campi procedunt. Veiens, multitudine abundans, post montes circummisit qui[5] inter dimicationem castra Romana aggrederentur. Trium populorum exercitus ita stetit instructus ut dextrum cornu Veientes, sinistrum Falisci tenerent, medii Fidenates essent. Dictator dextro cornu adversus Faliscos, sinistro contra Veientem Capitolinus Quinctius intulit[6] signa; ante mediam aciem cum equitatu magister equitum processit. Parumper silentium et quies fuit, Etruscis non, nisi cogerentur, pugnam inituris, et dictatore arcem Romanam respectante ut ex ea ab auguribus, simul atque aves rite admisissent, ex composito[7] tolleretur signum. Quod ubi conspexit, primos equites clamore sublato in hostem emisit. Secuta peditum acies ingenti vi conflixit. Nulla parte legiones Etruscae sustinuere impetum Romanorum. Eques maxime resistebat, equitumque longe fortissimus ipse rex certamen trahebat.

Erat tum inter equites Romanos tribunus quidam militum, A. Cornelius Cossus, eximia pulcritudine corporis, animo ac viribus par, memorque generis, quod amplissimum acceptum majus reliquit posteris. Is quum ad impetum Tolumnii trepidantes Romanas turmas videret, insignemque cum regio habitu tota acie volitantem cognosset; "Hiccine est," inquit, "ruptor foederis humani violatorque juris gentium;[3] jam ego hanc mactatam victimam, si modo sancti quidquam in terris esse di volunt, legatorum Manibus dabo." Calcaribus subditis infesto cuspide in unum fertur hostem. Quem quum equo dejecisset, confestim et ipse hasta innixus se in pedes excepit. Adsurgentem ibi regem umbone resupinat, repetitumque saepius cuspide ad terram adfixit. Tum exsangui detracta sunt spolia; caputque abscisum victor spiculo gerens terrore caesi regis hostes fudit. Ita equitum quoque fusa acies, quae una fecerat anceps certamen. Dictator legionibus fugatis instat, et ad castra compulsos caedit. Fidenatium plurimi locorum notitia effugere in montes. Cossus Tiberim cum equitatu transvectus ex agro Veientano ingentem praedam ad urbem detulit. Inter proelium et ad castra Romana pugnatum est adversus partem copiarum ab Tolumnio, ut ante dictum est, ad castra missam. Fabius Vibulanus vallum defendit, deinde porta principali dextra cum triariis egressus, hostes in vallum intentos repente invadit. Quo pavore injecto caedes minor, quia pauciores erant, fuga non minus trepida quam in acie fuit.

Omnibus locis re bene gesta, dictator senatus con-

sulto decretoque populi triumphans in urbem rediti.
Longe maximum triumphi spectaculum fuit Cossus,
spolia opima [9] regis interfecti gerens. In eum milites
carmina incondita cum Romulo aequantes canebant.
Spolia in aede Jovis Feretrii prope Romuli spolia,
quae prima opima appellata erant, cum solemni dedi-
catione fixit; averteratque in se a curru dictatoris
civium ora, et ejus diei gloriam prope solus tulerat.

XI. THE PROPHECY ABOUT THE ALBAN LAKE.

B.C. 397.

JAM Romani Veientesque in armis erant, tanta
ira odioque ut victis finem adesse appareret. Quum
spes major imperatoribus Romanis in obsidione quam
in oppugnatione esset, hibernacula etiam, res nova
militi Romano, aedificari coepta sunt,[1] consiliumque
erat hiemando continuare bellum. Prodigia interim
multa nuntiata sunt, quorum pleraque parum credita;
in unum curae omnium versae sunt, quod lacus in
Albano nemore sine ullis caelestibus aquis, causave
qua alia, quae rem miraculo eximeret, in altitudinem
insolitam crevit. Oratores ad oraculum Delphicum
missi rogatum quidnam eo prodigio di portenderent.
Sed propior interpres fatis oblatus est, senior quidam Veiens, qui inter cavillantes in stationibus ac
custodiis milites Romanos Etruscosque cecinit, priusquam ex lacu Albano aqua emissa foret, nunquam
potituros Veis Romanos. Quod primo sperni, deinde

agitari in sermonibus coeptum est, donec unus ex
statione Romana, proximum oppidanorum percunc-
tatus est quisnam is esset qui per ambages de lacu
Albano locutus esset. Postquam audivit haruspicem
esse, vatem ad colloquium elicuit. Quumque ambo
inermes sine ullo metu longius a suis progressi essent,
praevalens juvenis Romanus senem infirmum in omnium conspectu raptum ad suos transtulit. Qui
quum perductus ad imperatorem, inde Romam ad
senatum missus esset, rogantibus, quidnam id esset
quod de lacu Albano docuisset, respondit sic libris
fatalibus, sic disciplina Etrusca traditum esse, ut
quando aqua Albana abundasset, tum si eam Romanus
rite emisisset, victoriam de Veientibus dari; ante-
quam id fiat, deos moenia Veientium deserturos non
esse. Sed patres auctorem levem rati, nec super
tanta re satis fidum, decrevere legatos sortesque
oraculi Pythici expectandas.

Cetera bella, maximeque Veiens, incerti exitus
erant; jamque Romani, desperata ope humana, fata
et deos spectabant, quum legati ab Delphis venerunt
sortem oraculi afferentes congruentem responso captivi
vatis: "Romane, cave aquam Albanam lacu contineri,
cave in mare manare suo flumine sinas. Emissam per
agros rigabis, dissipatamque rivis extingues. Tum tu
audax insiste hostium muris; memento ex ea urbe,
quam per tot annos obsides, victoriam tibi his, quae
nunc panduntur, fatis datum. Bello perfecto donum
amplum victor ad mea templa portato."

XII. The Fall of Veii.
B.C. 396.

Jam ex lacu Albano aqua in agros emissa est, Veiosque fata appetebant. Igitur M. Furius Camillus, fatalis dux ad excidium illius urbis, dictator dictus magistrum equitum P. Cornelium Scipionem dixit. Omnia repente mutaverant[1] imperatore mutato : alia spes, alius animus hominum, fortuna quoque urbis alia videri. Camillus, delectu in certam diem indicto, ipse interim Veios ad confirmandos militum animos intercurrit; inde Romam ad conscribendum novum exercitum redit, nullo detractante militiam. Peregrina etiam juventus, Latini Hernicique operam suam pollicentes ad id bellum venere; quibus quum gratias in senatu egisset dictator, satis jam omnibus ad id bellum paratis, ludos magnos Veis captis se facturum ex senatus consulto vovit. Profectus cum exercitu ab urbe, primum cum Faliscis et Capenatibus signa confert. Omnia ibi summo consilio acta fortuna etiam secuta est. Non proelio tantum hostes fudit, sed castris quoque exuit, ingentique praeda est potitus. Inde Veios exercitus ductus est. Operum fuit omnium longe maximum ac laboriosissimum cuniculus in arcem hostium agi coeptus. Quod ne intermitteretur opus, neu sub terra continuus labor eosdem conficeret, in partes sex munitorum numerum divisit; senae horae in orbem operi attributae sunt, nocte ac die nunquam ante omissus labor quam in arcem viam facerent.

Dictator quum jam in manibus videret victoriam esse, urbem opulentissimam capi, tantumque praedae fore quantum non omnibus ante bellis fuisset, literas ad senatum misit: deum immortalium benignitate, suis consiliis, patientia militum Veios jam fore in potestate populi Romani; quid de praeda faciendum censerent? Duae senatum distinebant sententiae, altera senis P. Licini, cui placuit palam populo edici, ut qui particeps esse praedae vellet, in castra Veios iret; altera Appi Claudii qui auctor erat stipendii ex ea pecunia militi numerandi, ut eo minus tributi plebes conferret. Licini tutior visa sententia est quae popularem senatum faceret. Edictum itaque est, ad praedam Veientem, qui vellent, in castra ad dictatorem proficiscerentur.

Ingens profecta multitudo replevit castra. Tum dictator, quum edixisset ut arma milites caperent, "tuo ductu," inquit, "Pythice Apollo, tuoque numine instinctus, pergo ad delendam urbem Veios, tibique decimam partem praedae voveo." Inde ab omnibus locis urbem aggreditur quo minor periculi ab cuniculo ingruentis sensus hostibus esset. Veientes ignari se jam a suis vatibus, jam ab externis oraculis proditos esse, seque ultimum illum diem agere, neque suspicantes subrutis cuniculo moenibus arcem jam plenam hostium esse, in muros discurrunt.

Inseritur huic loco fabula: immolante rege Veientium, haruspicem dixisse ei victoriam dari qui exta ejus hostiae prosecuisset. Hanc vocem, in cuniculo exauditam, movisse Romanos milites ut aperto cuniculo exta raperent et ad dictatorem ferrent. Sed hanc fabulam neque affirmare neque refellere operae pretium est.² Cuniculus, delectis militibus eo tempore plenus, in aede Junonis, quae in Veientana arce erat, armatos repente edidit. Et pars hostes in muros aversos invadunt; pars claustra portarum revellunt; pars, quum ex tectis saxa tegulaeque a mulieribus ac servitiis jacerentur, inferunt ignes. Clamor omnia variis terrentium ac paventium vocibus, mixto mulierum ac puerorum ploratu complet. Momento temporis dejectis ex muro undique armatis, patefactisque portis, alii agmine irruunt, alii desertos scandunt muros; urbs hostibus impletur, omnibus locis pugnatur. Deinde multa jam edita caede senescit pugna, et dictator praecones edicere jubet ut ab inermi abstineatur.³ Is finis sanguinis fuit. Dedi inde inermes coepti, et ad praedam miles permissu dictatoris discurrit. Atque illa dies caede hostium ac direptione urbis opulentissimae est consumptus. Hic Veiorum occasus fuit, urbis opulentissimae Etrusci nominis,⁴ magnitudinem suam vel ultima clade indicantis, quod decem aestates hiemesque continuas circumsessa, quum plus cladium intulisset quam accepissset, postremo, jam fato quoque urgente, operibus non vi expugnata est.

Romam ut nuntiatum est Veios captos, velut ex insperato immensum gaudium fuit, et priusquam senatus decerneret, plena omnia templa Romanarum matrum grates dis agentium erant. Senatus in quatriduum supplicationes decernit. Adventus quoque dictatoris, omnibus ordinibus obviam effusis, et celebratior quam ullius umquam antea fuit, triumphusque consuetum honorandi illius diei modum excessit. Maxime **conspectus ipse est, curru equis** albis juncto urbem **invectus : idque parum non civile** modo sed humanum etiam [5] **visum est,** triumphusque **ob** eam unam **rem clarior quam** gratior **fuit. Tum** Junoni reginae templum **in** Aventino **locavit,** dedicavitque Matutae Matris. Atque his divinis **humanisque rebus gestis** dictatura **se abdicavit.**

XIII. The Coming of the Gauls.
B.C. 391.

Hoc **anno** M. Caedicius, **de plebe quidam,** nuntiavit **tribunis se** in nova **via, ubi nunc** sacellum est **supra** aedem Vestae vocem **noctis silentio audisse clariorem** humana, quae magistratibus **dici juberet** Gallos adventare. Id, ut **fit,** propter **auctoris** humilitatem spretum, et quod longinqua eoque **ignotior** gens erat. Neque deorum modo monita spreta sunt, sed humanam quoque **opem,**[1] **quae una** erat, **M. Furium Camillum** ab urbe amovere. **Qui, die** dicta ab **L.** Apuleio tribuno plebis propter **praedam** Veientanam, filio quoque adolescente per **idem tempus** orbatus, in exilium abiit, precatus ab **dis** immortalibus ut primo quoque tempore[2] **sui** desiderium civitati ingratae facerent.

Expulso cive, **quo** manente, si quidquam rerum

humanarum certum est, capi Roma non potuerat,
legati ab Clusinis veniunt auxilium adversus Gallos
petentes. Ea gens traditur dulcedine frugum,
maximeque vini, nova tum voluptate, capta Alpes
transisse agrosque ab Etruscis ante cultos occupavisse.
Clusini, novo bello exterriti, quum multitudinem,
quum formas hominum invisitatas cernerent, audirent-
que saepe ab iis cis et ultra Padum legiones Etruscorum fusas, quamquam adversus Romanos nullum iis
jus societatis amicitiaeve erat, legatos Romam, qui
auxilium ab senatu peterent, misere. De auxilio
nihil impetratum ; legati M. Fabii Ambusti filii
missi, qui nomine senatus populique Romani cum Gallis
agerent, ne socios populi Romani atque amicos oppug-
narent. Romanis eos, si res cogeret, tuendos esse ;
sed melius visum esse bellum ipsum amoveri, si posset,
et Gallos, novam gentem, pace potius cognosci quam
armis.

Mitis ea legatio, ni feroces legatos, Gallisque magis
quam Romanis similes habuisset. Quibus, postquam
mandata ediderunt in concilio Gallorum, hoc responsum datum est. Etsi novum nomen audiant Romanorum, tamen credere viros fortes esse, quorum auxilium
a Clusinis in re trepida sit imploratum ; et quoniam
legatione adversus se maluerint quam armis tueri
socios, ne se quidem pacem quam illi afferant aspernari,
si Gallis agro egentibus, quem latius possideant quam
colant Clusini, partem finium concedant. Aliter
pacem impetrari non posse. Se et responsum Clusin-

orum coram Romanis accipere velle, et, si negetur ager, coram iisdem Romanis dimicaturos, ut domum nuntiare possent quantum Galli ceteros mortales virtute praestarent. Mox accensis utrimque animis ad arma discurritur et proelium conseritur. Ibi legati contra jus gentium arma capiunt. Nec id clam esse potuit, quum ante signa Etruscorum tres fortissimi nobilissimique Romanae juventutis pugnarent. Quin etiam Q. Fabius, evectus extra aciem, ducem Gallorum equo in ipsa signa Etruscorum incursantem per latus transfixum hasta occidit. Spolia ejus legentem Galli agnovere, perque totam aciem Romanum legatum esse signum datum est. Omissa inde in Clusinos ira receptui canunt [3] minitantes Romanis. Erant qui extemplo Romam eundum esse censerent; vicere seniores, ut legati prius mitterentur questum injurias postulatumque ut pro jure gentium violato Fabii dederentur. Quum legati Gallorum ea, sicut erant mandata, exposuissent, Fabiorum factum senatui non placebat, et jus postulare barbari videbantur. Sed ambitio obstabat ne id quod placebat decernerent in tantae nobilitatis viris. Itaque, ne penes ipsos culpa esset cladis forte Gallico bello acceptae, cognitionem de postulatis Gallorum ad populum rejiciunt. Ibi tanto plus gratia atque opes valebant ut ii quorum de poena agebatur, tribuni militum consulari potestate in sequentem annum crearentur. Quo facto Galli, haud secus quam dignum erat infensi, bellum palam minantes ad suos redeunt.

XIV. The Battle of the Allia.

B.C. 390.

Galli, postquam accepere honorem habitum viola-
toribus juris gentium, elusamque legationem suam
esse, flagrantes ira, cujus impotens est gens, confestim signis convulsis citato agmine iter ingrediuntur.
Quum urbes exterritae ad arma concurrerent, fugaque
agrestium fieret, Romam se ire magno clamore signi-
ficabant, quacumque ibant equis virisque late fusis
immensum spatium obtinentes. Sed antecedente fama
nuntiisque Clusinorum, plurimum terroris Romam
hostium celeritas tulit, quibus, exercitu raptim ducto,
aegre ad undecimum lapidem occursum est, qua
flumen Allia, Crustuminis montibus praealto defluens
alveo haud multum infra viam Tiberino amni miscetur.
Jam omnia contra circaque hostium plena erant, et
gens in vanos tumultus nata truci cantu clamoribusque
variis cuncta horrendo sono compleverant.

Tribuni militum non loco castris ante capto, non
praemunito vallo, quo receptus esset, instruunt aciem
in cornua diductam[1] ne multitudine hostium circum-
veniri possent. Nec tamen aequari frontes poterant,
quum extenuando mediam aciem infirmam et vix
cohaerentem haberent. Editus erat ab dextera locus
quem subsidiariis repleri placuit; eaque res ut initium
pavoris ac fugae, sic una salus fugientibus fuit. Nam
Brennus, Gallorum regulus, in paucitate hostium

artem [2] maxime timens, in subsidiarios signa convertit,
haud dubius, si eos loco depulisset facilem in aequo
campo victoriam fore. Adeo non fortuna modo sed
ratio etiam cum barbaris stabat.[3] In altera acie nihil
simile Romanis, non apud duces, non apud milites
erat. Pavor fugaque occupaverat animos, et tanta
omnium rerum oblivio ut multo major pars Veios
quam recto itinere Romam ad conjuges ac liberos
fugerent. Parumper subsidiarios tutatus est locus;
in reliqua acie simul atque auditus est hostium
clamor, non modo non tentato certamine sed ne
clamore quidem reddito, integri intactique fugerunt.
Nec ulla caedes pugnantium fuit; terga caesa suo
ipsorum certamine in turba fugam impedientium.
Circa ripam Tiberis, quo armis abjectis totum sinistrum cornu defugit, magna strages facta est; multos-
que imperitos nandi aut loricis aliisque tegminibus
impeditos hausere gurgites. Maxima tamen pars
incolumis Veios perfugit, unde ne nuntius quidem
cladis Romam missus est. Ab dextro cornu, quod
procul a flumine et magis sub monte steterat, Romam
omnes petiere, et ne clausis quidem portis urbis in
arcem confugerunt. Gallos quoque, velut obstupe-
factos, miraculum victoriae tam repentinae tenuit.
Et ipsi pavore defixi primum steterunt velut ignari
quid accidisset; deinde insidias vereri; postremo
caesorum spolia legere, armorumque cumulos, ut
mos iis est, coacervare. Tum demum, postquam
nihil usquam hostile cernebatur, viam ingressi

c

haud multo ante solis occasum ad urbem Romam
perveniunt.

XV. The Burning of Rome by the Gauls.
b.c. 390.

Romani, quum major pars ex acie Veios petisset,
neminem superesse rati praeter eos qui Romam refug-
erant, totam urbem lamentis impleverunt. Privatos
deinde luctus stupefecit publicus pavor, postquam
hostes adesse nuntiatum est. Mox ululatus cantusque
dissonos barbarorum circa moenia vagantium audie-
bant. Quum spes nulla esset, tam parva relicta manu,
urbem defendi posse, placuit cum conjugibus ac liberis
juventutem militarem senatusque robur in arcem
Capitoliumque concedere, armisque et frumento collato
deos hominesque et nomen Romanum defendere. Si
arx Capitoliumque, sedes deorum, si senatus, caput
publici consilii, si militaris juventus superesset, levem
esse jacturam seniorum turbaeque in urbe utique peri-
turae. Et quo id aequiore animo plebis multitudo
ferret, senes consulares dicebant se simul cum illis obi-
turos, nec his corporibus, quibus arma ferre non possent, inopiam armatorum oneraturos.

Inde seniores morti destinati agmen juvenum in
Capitolium prosequebantur, eorum virtuti fortunam
urbis commendantes. Plebis maxima pars, quam nec
capere tam exiguus collis, nec in tanta frumenti inopia
alere poterat, ex urbe effusa, uno agmine Janiculum

petiit. Inde pars per agros dilapsi, pars urbes petunt
finitimas, sine ullo duce aut consensu, suum quisque
consilium exsequentes. Flamen interea Quirinalis
virginesque Vestales quae sacrorum secum ferre non
poterant in sacello prope flaminis aedes defodiunt,
cetera, partito **inter se** onere, via quae ducit ad Janiculum ferunt. Eas quum L. Albinius, de plebe
Romana homo, conspexisset, plaustro conjugem ac
liberos habens, irreligiosum ratus sacerdotes **pub-
licos sacraque populi Romani pedibus ire ferrique,**[1] se
autem ac suos in **vehiculo** conspici, **descendere uxorem**
ac pueros jussit, virgines sacraque in plaustrum **im-
posuit** et Caere pervexit.

Romae interim, **omnibus jam ad tuendam arcem**
paratis, turba **seni**orum domos regressa adventum
hostium obstinato ad mortem animo expectabat.
Qui eorum curules gesserant magistratus, augustis-
sima veste vestiti medio aedium eburneis sellis
sedere. Galli ingressi postero die urbem patente
Collina porta in forum perveniunt, circumferentes
oculos ad templa deum, arcemque solam belli speciem
tenentem. Inde modico relicto praesidio, ne quis
ex arce impetus fieret, dilapsi ad praedam, vacuis **viis**
pars in proxima tecta ruunt, pars ultima petunt.
Inde rursus ipsa solitudine exterriti, ne qua fraus
hostilis vagos exciperet, in forum ac propinqua foro
loca redibant ; ubi plebis aedificiis obseratis, patenti-
bus atriis principum, major prope cunctatio tenebat
aperta quam clausa invadendi. Venerabundi intue-

bantur viros in aedium vestibulis sedentes, qui
praeter ornatum habitumque, majestate etiam orisque
gravitate dis simillimi videbantur.   Ad eos velut
simulacra versi quum starent, M. Papirius unus ex
senatoribus Gallum barbam suam permulcentem sci-
pione eburneo percussisse dicitur ; atque ab eo initium
caedis ortum, ceteros in sedibus suis trucidatos.   Post
principum caedem nulli deinde mortalium parcitur,
tecta diripiuntur, exhaustis ignes injiciuntur.

XVI. The Siege of the Citadel, and Defeat of the Gauls by Camillus.   b.c. 390.

Galli, quum inter incendia ac ruinas captae urbis
nihil superesse praeter armatos hostes viderent, impetum in arcem facere statuunt.   Prima luce signo dato
multitudo omnis in foro instruitur ; inde clamore sublato ac testudine [1] facta subeunt.   Adversus quos
Romani, stationibus ad omnes aditus firmatis, scan-
dere hostem sinunt ; quo magis in arduum successerit,
eo facilius per proclive pelli posse rati.   Medio fere
clivo restitere, atque inde ex loco superiore, qui prope
sua sponte in hostem inferebat, impetu facto Gallos
tante strage ac ruina fudere, ut nunquam postea tale
genus pugnae tentaverint.

Omissa itaque spe per vim atque arma subeundi, ob-
sidionem parant.   Exercitu diviso partim per finitimos
populos praedari placuit, partim obsideri arcem, ut

obsidentibus frumentum populatores agrorum praebe-
rent. Proficiscentes ab urbe Gallos fortuna ipsa
Ardeam, ubi Camillus exulabat, duxit ; hic, maestior
ibi publica fortuna quam sua, repente audit Gallorum
exercitum adventare, atque de eo pavidos Ardeates
consulere. Quum se in mediam contionem intulisset:
"Ardeates," inquit, "fortuna vobis jam oblata est et
pro tantis populi Romani beneficiis gratiae referendae
et huic urbi decus belli ingens pariendi. Qui effuso
agmine adventant, gens est cui natura corpora animos-
que magna magis quam firma dederit. **Eo in** certa-
mina plus terroris quam virium ferunt. Argumento [2]
sit clades Romana ; patentem cepere urbem ; ex **arce**
Capitolioque his exigua manu resistitur. **Jam** obsidionis taedio victi abscedunt, vagique per agros palan-
tur. Cibo vinoque repleti, ubi nox appetit, **prope**
rivos aquarum sine stationibus ac custodiis passim
ferarum ritu sternuntur. Si vobis in animo est
moenia vestra tueri, prima vigilia capite arma, meque
ad caedem, non ad pugnam, sequimini."

Omnibus persuasum erat tantum bello virum neminem eo tempore esse. Dato itaque signo, primae silentio
noctis ad portas Camillo adfuere. Egressi haud procul urbe, sicut praedictum erat, castra Gallorum intuta
neglectaque ab omni parte nacti cum ingenti clamore
invadunt. Nusquam proelium, omnibus locis caedes
est ; corpora nuda et somno soluta trucidantur. Ex-
tremos tamen, e cubilibus excitos, pavor in fugam et
quosdam in ipsum hostem tulit. Magna pars in

agrum Antiatem delati, incursione ab oppidanis facta circumveniuntur.

Veis interim non animi solum sed etiam vires indies crescebant, et maturum[3] jam videbatur patriam ex hostium manibus eripi. Sed corpori valido caput deerat Locus ipse admonebat Camilli, et magna pars militum erat qui ejus ductu auspicioque res prospere gesserant. Consensu omnium placuit ab Ardea Camillum acciri, sed senatu, qui Romae esset, antea consulto. Ingenti periculo per hostium custodias transeundum erat. Ad eam rem Pontius Cominius, inpiger juvenis, operam pollicitus cortici incubans secundo Tiberi ad urbem defertur. Inde per praeruptum saxum in Capitolium evadit, et ad magistratus ductus mandata exercitus edit. Accepto inde senatus consulto ut Camillus, jussu populi de exilio revocatus, dictator diceretur, eadem degressus Veios contendit, legatique Ardeam ad Camillum missi Veios eum perduxere.

Dum haec Veis agebantur, interim arx Romae Capitoliumque in ingenti periculo fuit. Namque Galli, vestigio notato humano, qua nuntius a Veis pervenerat, nocte sublustri primo inermem, qui tentaret viam, praemisere: inde arma tradentes, atque alii alios trahentes sublevantesque, tanto silentio in summum evasere, ut non custodes solum fallerent, sed ne canes quidem, animal ad nocturnos strepitus sollicitum, excitarent. Anseres non fefellere, quibus Junoni sacris in summa cibi inopia abstinebatur.[4] Quae res saluti fuit; namque clangore eorum alarumque crepitu excitus M. Manlius qui triennio ante consul fuerat, vir bello egregius, armis arreptis ceterosque simul ad arma ciens vadit, et dum ceteri trepidant, Gallum qui jam in summo constiterat, umbone ictum deturbat. Cujus casus quum proximos Gallorum sterneret, trepidantes alios, armisque omissis saxa manibus amplexos, trucidat Manlius. Jamque et alii congregati telis missilibusque saxis proturbare hostes, totaque prolapsa acies in praeceps deferri. Sedato deinde tumultu reliquum noctis quieti datum est. Luce orta, vocatis ad concilium militibus, Manlius primum ob virtutem laudatus ; tum vigiles ejus loci qua fefellerat ascendens hostis citati. Quibus omnibus culpam in unum vigilem conjicientibus, Q. Sulpicius, tribunus militum, reum ejus noxae approbantibus cunctis de saxo dejecit. Inde intentiores utriuque custodiae esse, et apud Gallos quia vulgatum erat inter Veios Romamque nuntios commeare, et apud Romanos ab nocturni periculi memoria.

Sed ante omnia obsidionis bellique mala, fames utrumque exercitum urgebat. Indutiae deinde factae, et colloquia permissu imperatorum habita ; in quibus quum Galli famem Romanis objicerent, eaque necessitate ad deditionem eos vocarent, dicitur avertendae ejus opinionis causa multis locis panis de Capitolio jactatus esse in hostium stationes. Sed jam neque dissimulari neque ferri ultra fames poterat. Itaque, dum dictator exercitum parat quo haud impar adoriatur hostes, interim Capitolinus exercitus, stationibus

vigiliisque fessus, fame victus, spe postremo deficiente,
et armis infirma corpora prope obruentibus, vel dedi
vel redimi se jussit. Tum senatus habitus, tribun-
isque militum negotium datum ut paciscerentur.
Inde inter Q. Sulpicium tribunum militum, et Bren-
num regulum Gallorum colloquio transacta res est et
mille pondo⁵ auri pretium populi factum. Rei per se
foedissimae adjecta est indignitas : pondera a Gallis
allata iniqua, et tribuno recusante, gladius ab insolenti
Gallo ponderi additus, auditaque ea vox intoleranda
Romanis. " Vae victis ! "

Sed diique et homines prohibuere redemptos vivere
Romanos. Nam forte, priusquam infanda merces
perficeretur, dictator intervenit, auferrique aurum de
medio, et Gallos submoveri jubet. Quum illi reni-
tentes pactos dicerent esse, negat eam pactionem
ratam esse, quae postquam ipse dictator creatus esset
injussu suo facta esset : denuntiatque Gallis ut se ad
proelium expediant. Suos arma aptare ferroque non
auro recuperare patriam jubet. Instruit deinde aciem
in semirutae solo urbis, et omnia quae arte belli suis
secunda parari poterant providet. Galli nova re tre-
pidi arma capiunt, iraque magis quam consilio in
Romanos incurrunt. Jam verterat⁶ fortuna, jam
deorum opes humanaque consilia rem Romanam ad-
juvabant. Igitur primo concursu haud majore momento fusi sunt Galli quam quo ad Alliam vicerant.
Justiore altero deinde proelio ad octavum lapidem
Gabina via, quo se ex fuga contulerant, ductu ejusdem

Camilli vincuntur. Ibi magna caedes facta. Castra capiuntur et ne nuntius quidem cladis relictus. Dictator recuperata ex hostibus patria triumphans in urbem redit, interque jocos militares Romulus ac pater patriae conditorque alter urbis haud vanis laudibus appellabatur.

GENERAL NOTE.—The chief difficulty which will be found by boys beginning this book will probably be the order of words in the sentence. The subject will constantly come in the middle or at the end of the sentence, and the verb, object, etc., in rather unexpected places. Careful parsing will, however, soon get over the difficulty.

NOTES.

I.

1. **plus posse** = to be stronger.

2. **Vestalem.** The priestesses of Vesta were forbidden to marry, so Amulius hoped that **his** niece would have **no children who** might overthrow him.

3. **Faustulo, dat., in** apposition to *huic*.

4. **id ipsum.** The meaning is that the time when Faustulus found the twins agreed with the date at which the royal children had been **exposed.**

5. **Numitori,** indirect object to *tetigerat*.

6. **re.** *Res* is often used in Latin where we should use a less **vague** word. In translating, consider what particular 'thing' is meant, and choose a suitable English word.

II.

1. **mollirent, darent,** indirect command.

2. **quum ... tum** = both ... and.

III.

1. **agunt.** *Cum aliquo agere ut ...* = to induce a man to ...

2. **consertis** manibus. *Manus conserere* = to come to close quarters.

3. **eo ... quo** = in proportion as.

43

V.

1. **indignitatem.** The fact of the city being besieged was felt as an insult by the Romans.

2. **ignaris omnibus,** abl. abs.

3. **comprehensum retraxerunt.** Translate the participle and verb by two verbs, "seized and dragged back."

4. **hostis hostem.** In English we should omit *hostis.*

VI.

1. **ad = on.**

2. **concursum est,** impersonal.

3. **quem ... illum.** In Latin the relative clause often comes before the antecedent. Change the order in translating.

4. See V., note 3.

VII.

1. **quanti.** Gen. of price.

2. **jura.** The plebeians had lately won the right of having their own magistrates, called tribunes, to protect them against the patrician consuls.

3. **diem dicere alicui,** "to name a day for a man," i.e. to appoint a day for his trial ; to bring him to trial.

4. **referre** = to refer the matter to the Senate, to consult the Senate.

5. **alii ... alio** = some say by one, some by another.

VIII.

In this passage, and especially at the beginning, the sentences are very short and terse. In compound tenses the auxiliary verb is constantly omitted, a favourite practice with Livy, for which you must always be prepared.

1. **Patres conscripti,** i.e. *patres et conscripti.* This was the regular form used in addressing the Senate. The *Patres* were the senators in the time of the kings. After the expulsion of the Tarquins new senators were added, who were called *conscripti,* "the chosen ones."

2. Jano. The temple of the god Janus was a covered **pass-age** with a door at each end. Hence any arched passage **came** to be called by this name.

3. infesta. The opposite to *tuta*.

4. collatis signis. *Conferre signa* means "to bring the standards together," i.e. "to fight at close quarters."

5. maximum auxilium. The reference is chiefly to Q. Fabius Maximus, who saved Rome after the battle of Lake Trasimene in the second Punic war. Ovid refers to him more distinctly in his account of the destruction of the Fabii—

> "Nam **puer** impubes et adhuc non utilis armis
>   Unus de Fabia gente relictus **erat.**
> Scilicet ut posses olim tu, Maxime, nasci,
>   Cui **res** cunctando restituenda **foret.**"

IX.

1. placuisset. "It had been decided."

2. aetate militari. Between 17 and 43.

3. unde = *ex eo loco qui.*

4. alibi … alibi. In the one place … in the other.

5. orare, historical infinitive.

6. jugum. To pass under the yoke was a sign of defeat and submission.

7. praedae, dat. of purpose.

8. habitus. *Senatum habere* = to hold a meeting of the Senate.

X.

1. tertium. Here used adverbially.

2. Faliscus. Singular for plural: a frequent use in Livy.

3. poscere. Historical infinitive.

4. bina castra. *Castra* being a pl. noun requires the distributive numeral.

5. qui. The antecedent must be supplied.

6. intulit signa. *Signa inferre* = to advance to the attack.

7. ex composito. "According to agreement."

8. **violator**, etc.   Because he had urged the men of Fidenae to kill the ambassadors.

9. **spolia opima.**   These were said to be won when the Roman general killed the general of the enemy.   Cossus according to Livy was not the general, but other accounts say that he was consul that year.

XI.

1. **coepta sunt**, passive, because the dependent infinitive is passive.

XII.

1. **mutaverant**, intransitive.

2. **operae pretium est.**   "It is worth while."

3. **abstineatur**, impersonal.   Why?

4. **nominis.**   'The Etruscan name' means 'the Etruscan race.'

5. **civile ... humanum.**   The meaning is that Camillus took more upon him than became a citizen or even a man; i.e. he seemed to be making himself equal to a king, or even to the gods.

XIII.

1. **humanam opem.**   In apposition to *Camillum.*

2. **primo quoque tempore** = as soon as possible.

3. **receptui canere.**   "To sound a retreat," lit. to play (on the trumpet) for a retreat.

XIV.

1. **in cornua diductum**, i.e. stretched out so as to cover as much space as possible.

2. **artem.**   "Stratagem."

3. **cum C. stabat.**   "Was on the side of."

XV.

1. **ire ferrique.**   *Ire* refers to the priests, *ferri* to the sacred vessels.

XVI.

1. **testudine.** A protection formed by the soldiers **holding their** shields locked closely together over their heads. Translate here "**with shields** locked."

2. **argumento.** Dat. of purpose.

3. **maturum videbatur.** "It seemed high time."

4. abstinebatur. Impersonal.

5. **pondo.** Originally **an** adverb meaning "**by weight.**" So *mille librae pondo* **would** mean "1,000 lbs. by weight." The word *librae* being **omitted,** *pondo* **comes to be used** as an indeclinable noun meaning "pounds."

6. **verteret.** Intransitive.

Note.—The English index will generally, but not always, enable you to find idiomatic Latin words and phrases to translate the English. Sometimes the proper phrase can only be found in the Latin passage to which the exercise belongs. Such phrases are, in the earlier exercises, printed in italics.

Words to be omitted are enclosed in round brackets ( ), hints for translation in square brackets [ ].

EXERCISES.

I.

1. The **king** of Alba has two sons.
2. By the will **of his** father the kingdom was left **to** Numitor.
3. As the **Tiber had** overflowed its banks, they could **not** approach **the** stream.
4. **Those to whom** the children have been given will **not perform** the king's command.
5. They say that the shepherd gave **the boys to his** wife to **be** brought up.
6. The robbers, having lost **their booty,** made an attack upon the **two** young men.
7. Faustulus believed that the youths whom he had taken up were the grandsons of **the** king.
8. When Numitor **heard** that the twins had **not been killed, he** recognised Remus **as** his grandson.
9. With the help of Remus [Remus helping] Amulius is slain, and the royal power is conferred upon Numitor.

10. Through desire of founding a new city, Romulus and Remus went away from Alba.

11. An omen is said to have come to Remus first.

12. When Remus had been killed, Romulus gave his name to the new city.

II.

1. On account of the scarcity of women the Romans sent ambassadors and sought intermarriage with their neighbours.

2. When the games were proclaimed many men came to Rome.

3. All the Sabines were present from desire of seeing the spectacle.

4. When the signal was given by the king, the Romans seized the maidens.

5. The parents of the Sabine women roused their neighbours to *engage in battle* with the Romans.

6. When war had been begun by the Sabines, peace was made by the women who had been carried off [*perf. part.*]

7. They begged their fathers and husbands not to engage in battle.

8. When the treaty was made the leaders united the two kingdoms.

III.

1. It is well known that war arose between the Romans and Albans.

2. It is uncertain whether the Horatii were Romans or Albans.

3. A treaty is made on this condition [*lex*] that the nation whose citizens **conquer in** the fight shall rule over the other.

4. The three young men on each side took their arms and *came to close quarters.*

5. When **two** Romans had been **killed, and the three** Albans wounded, he who **survived of the** Romans *took to flight.*

6. **This he did** that he might separate his enemies.

7. When he had fled *some distance*, he saw his enemies pursuing *far apart.*

8. He then made an attack on them **and killed them one by one** [*singuli* adj.].

9. On account of their wounds **one** brother could **not** bring aid to the other [*one brother* . . . **the** *other* = *frater* . . . *frater*].

10. Horatius, having **spoiled the** Albans, was received with great **joy by the citizens.**

IV.

1. Porsena promised to come to Rome with his army, that **the** Tarquins might **not** *live in exile.*

2. Horatius held the foe **at bay** while the citizens were breaking **down the** bridge.

3. When his companions had returned into the city Horatius challenged the enemy to battle.

4. The enemy, moved by shame, made a rush at Horatius.

5. But when the bridge was broken, he jumped down into the river and swam across unhurt to his companions.

6. The grateful citizens placed a statue of Horatius in the city, and gave him land as a reward [*praemium*] for his courage.

V

1. Mucius feared that Porsena would take the city by siege.

2. He determined to penetrate into the camp of the enemy in order to avenge this insult.

3. When the senators had heard the matter, they approved of the design of Mucius.

4. He said that he would kill the king if he could.

5. But when he came to the camp, he feared to inquire which was the king, which the secretary.

6. (When) seized by the guards he said that he was a Roman, that he was called C. Mucius.

7. (He said) that he and all the Roman youths wished to kill the king.

8. When Mucius had shown that he did not fear pain, the king ordered him to be sent away unharmed.

9. Mucius then said that many Roman youths had conspired to kill the king.

10. The Romans gave to Mucius the surname of Scaevola.

VI.

1. The Romans met the army of the Latins at Lake Regillus.
2. The battle was even fiercer because they had heard that the Tarquins were among the enemy.
3. It is well known that none of the leaders escaped without a wound.
4. The Latins *rescued* from the battle Tarquinius (who was) wounded by the dictator.
5. When the battle was renewed the exiles made an attack upon the Roman line.
6. Valerius, having put spurs to his horse, was carried into the enemy's line.
7. The dictator says that he will *treat as an enemy* the man whom he sees flying.
8. The Romans turned against the enemy, and the Latin general was killed by T. Herminius.
9. When the cavalry had *dismounted*, they routed the Latins.
10. The Romans pursued the fugitives [*pres. part.*] with such eagerness that they took the camp.

VII.

1. The army of the Volscians attacked the Romans while they were besieging the city.
2. When Marcius with his men had broken into the city, he killed many of the townsmen and set fire to the buildings.
3. It was asked in the senate *at what price* corn should be sold.

4. The opinion of Coriolanus was that the people should restore to the patricians their former right, if they wished corn to be given to them.

5. For this reason Marcius was *put on his trial* by the tribunes.

6. When he had gone away into exile he was kindly received by the Volscians.

7. He was made general that he might take away towns from the Romans and hand them over to the Volscians.

8. The patricians were united with the plebeians through fear *of a foreign foe.*

9. The consuls were compelled by the mass of the people to refer the matter to the senate.

10. Coriolanus replied that he would not treat about peace unless the Romans gave back their lands to the Volscians.

11. Rome was saved not by the arms of men but by the prayers of women.

12. It was announced to Coriolanus that his mother and wife and children were present.

13. His mother asked him whether she had come to her son or to an enemy.

14. Coriolanus, moved by the prayers of the women, went away from Rome with his army.

VIII.

1. The Fabii said that the war with Veii did not need a large army ; let the Romans wage other wars, and give to them this one.

2. The consul, who was himself a Fabius, ordered **the** Fabii to **be present,** armed, **on** the following day.

3. **3.** When the consul went out all his clan were standing *in marching order.*

4. **4.** A great crowd followed the Fabii as they **went** [going] through the city.

5. **5.** When they had reached the river Cremera, they found a suitable place for fortifying the camp.

6. **6.** When the **Fabii had** made everything **insecure for** the enemy. **the Veientines attacked their camp.**

7. **7.** The consul did **not give the enemy room** for extending their **line.**

8. **8.** The enemy soon repented of the peace which they had obtained.

9. The Fabii, having made many raids upon **the** territory of the Etruscans, also fought **with** them hand **to** hand in *battle array.*

10. It seemed to the Veientines that the Romans ought **to** be taken by an ambush.

11. **11.** The Fabii, thinking that the enemy could not withstand **them,** *made a raid* upon cattle seen at a distance.

12. **12.** Being hemmed in by the enemy, they forced their way **to a hill.**

13. When the Fabii were slain their camp was *taken by storm.*

14. Three hundred and six perished, and one boy was left.

IX.

1. When the daring of the enemy had increased, they attacked the consul's army by night.

2. The horsemen announced that the camp was surrounded by the Aequi.

3. It was therefore decided that Cincinnatus should be appointed dictator.

4. When the messengers sent by the senate had explained the cause of (their) coming, Cincinnatus set out for Rome.

5. He was there received by his kinsmen and friends.

6. Next day the shops were shut throughout the whole city, and all who were of military age were present in the field of Mars.

7. When they had reached Algidus the soldiers were *placed round* the enemy's camp.

8. The shout raised by the dictator's army was heard in the Roman camp.

9. It caused great joy to the soldiers because they knew that help was at hand.

10. While the Aequi were fighting with the consul, they were shut in by the dictator.

11. The enemy begged the dictator not to kill them all, (but) to let them lay down their arms and return home.

12. He replied that they must be sent under the yoke, and that then they should go away unharmed.

13. When the enemy had been sent away, all the plunder was given by Cincinnatus to his own soldiers.

14. Cincinnatus entered Rome *in triumph*, and before his chariot went the leaders of the Acqui [*and . . . his*, rel. pron.].

X.

1. Ambassadors sent from Rome were killed **by the** men of Fidenae, **who** had revolted.

2. War having arisen, **the consul** gained a victory but lost many citizens.

3. The dictator, a man skilled **in** war, came **to** the rescue.

4. He said that he **would not descend into the** plains until the army of the enemy arrived.

5. Some of the enemy demanded battle, others wished to prolong **the war.**

6. Although this plan **was more** pleasing to the king, nevertheless he announced that he would fight at daybreak.

7. The Etruscans said **that** they would **not begin the battle** unless they were compelled.

8. When **the** Roman legions were sent against the Etruscans, the infantry could not withstand their onset.

9. **The battle** was prolonged chiefly by the cavalry, **of whom** the **king** himself was by far the **bravest.**

10. The king was hurled to the ground by Cossus, who killed him and tore off the spoils.

11. When the king was killed the enemy were routed.

12. A vast quantity of plunder was brought to Rome by Cossus.

13. When the dictator triumphed [*abl. abs.*] Cossus bore the spoils of the slain king, and gained [*fero*] nearly all the glory of the victory.

XI.

1. The Romans hoped to take Veii by siege.

2. In this war they began to build winter-quarters for the soldiers.

3. When the Alban lake had risen to an unusual height, envoys were sent to Delphi.

4. But before they returned an old man of Veii explained [*expono*] what the portent foreboded.

5. A young Roman seized the old prophet after he had enticed him into a conversation.

6. The senate asked him what he had said about the Alban lake.

7. He replied that the gods would not desert Veii until the Romans had let out the water from the lake.

8. The senate ordained that the return of the ambassadors must be awaited.

9. *Answer was made* [impersonal] by the oracle that the Romans would take Veii if they let out the water over the fields.

XII.

1. M. Furius Camillus was appointed dictator to carry on the war with Veii.

2. When he had returned from Veii to Rome he enrolled a new army.

3. The Latins and Hernicans **also** promised **to come to** the war.

4. When the dictator had prepared everything **for** the war, he set out from Rome and routed **the** enemy in battle.

5. The general began to dig a mine under ground **into the** enemy's citadel.

6. The *workers* **were** divided into six detachments, **so** that they might not be worn out by **toil.**

7. When the dictator saw that he should soon take the city, he asked the senate what was to be done about the plunder.

8. It was decided [*placere*] that that plunder should be given to those who chose [*volo*] to go to Veii.

9. The consul attacked the city from all sides, that the enemy might not know where the greatest danger was.

10. The Veientines did not know that their walls were undermined by the Romans.

11. There is a story that the soldiers **in** the mine heard the voice of the soothsayer ;

12. And that they seized the entrails **of** the victim and carried **them to** the dictator.

13. When the **soldiers** had **set fire to** the city, the wailing **of women and children** was heard.

14. The gates were opened and **the** city filled with armed men

15. When the city was taken, the soldiers ran off to the plunder.

16. Thus the city was taken *after a siege of* [having been besieged] ten years.

17. When *news reached Rome* that Veii was taken, the Roman matrons gave thanks to the gods.

18. The triumph of the dictator was more brilliant than (that) of anyone before.

XIII.

1. It was announced to the tribunes that a certain man had heard a voice which said that the Gauls were at hand.

2. At this time Camillus, *being accused* by Apuleius, went into exile.

3. The Gauls crossed the Alps that they might seize the lands of Italy.

4. The men of Clusium sent ambassadors to Rome to beg for aid against the Gauls.

5. Ambassadors sent by the senate said that the people of Clusium were allies of the Roman people.

6. The Gauls, because they believed that the Romans were brave men, did not scorn peace with them.

7. The answer of the people of Clusium was given in the presence of the Romans.

8. They said that they would not give the land which the Gauls asked for.

9. When the battle was begun the Roman ambassadors fought in the army of the people of Clusium, and one of them slew with his spear a chieftain of the Gauls.

10. The Gauls, when they had recognised Fabius, **sent** ambassadors **to** Rome to demand that **he** should **be given up to them.**

11. When the matter had been referred to the people, the Fabii **were** appointed tribunes of the soldiers **for the** following **year.**

XIV.

1. **The** Gauls having **entered on their march** reached the river Allia with great speed.

2. **When** the tribes [*gens*] **of** Etruria heard **that the** Gauls were at hand, they ran **to** arms.

3. The Romans, having hastily **levied an army, met** the enemy at **the eleventh** milestone **from the city.**

4. The Roman leader neither **chose a** position **for** the camp, nor fortified entrenchments.

5. The centre of **the** Roman line was weak, because they had stretched **it** out that the enemy might **not** surround them.

6. The **Gauls first** made an attack **upon** the reserves, that **they** might have an easier victory in the plain.

7. Such panic seized the minds of **the** Romans that they fled *without attempting* battle [abl. abs.].

8. Many while crossing the **river** Tiber were swept away by the eddies.

9. Those who escaped to Veii did not even send news of the disaster **to** Rome

10. The Gauls, amazed by so sudden a victory, at
    first feared an ambush, then having gathered
    the spoils and heaped up a pile of arms, they
    made their way to Rome.

XV.

1. The Romans knew by the discordant cries of the
   barbarians that the enemy were at hand.

2. They had no hope that they could defend the city,
   as so few of the soldiers were left.

3. When they had determined that the citadel alone
   must be defended, they collected arms and
   corn.

4. The older men said that they would perish with
   the city, that they might not *be a burden* [*oneri
   esse*] to the armed men.

5. As the Capitol could not hold all the people, the
   greater part *fled for refuge* [*confugere*] to Janiculum.

6. The priests and Vestal virgins, carrying with them
   the sacred (vessels), went to Caere.

7. The old men awaited the arrival of the Gauls
   each sitting in the entrance of his own house

8. When the Gauls had entered the city and reached
   the forum they separated to plunder.

9. When they saw the men sitting on ivory chairs
   they at first thought they were gods.

10. But when Papirius struck one of the Gauls with his staff, all the old men were slaughtered, and the houses *were set on fire.*

XVI.

1. The Gauls, in order that they might get possession of the whole city, made an attack upon the citadel.

2. The Romans allowed them to climb to the middle of the slope.

3. The Gauls were routed with such slaughter that they never afterwards attempted to get up by force.

4. They sent part of their army to plunder through the neighbouring country.

5. Camillus said that a chance was now offered to the Ardeates of *showing gratitude* to the Romans.

6. He said that the bodies of the Gauls were large but not strong, and that they could be conquered by a small force.

7. He begged them to take arms and follow him to battle.

8. They found the camp of the Gauls unprotected and without guards

9. When many of the Gauls had been killed, a great part also were surrounded by the enemy.

10. The Romans who were at Veii decided that Camillus should be summoned from Ardea.

11. A young man was sent to Rome to consult the senate on this matter.

12. He was carried down the Tiber and reached the Capitol.

13. The senate decreed that Camillus should be appointed dictator.

14. Meanwhile the Gauls, pulling each other up, reached the top of the Capitol by night.

15. The geese sacred to Juno saved [were for a safety to] the citadel.

16. Manlius, aroused from sleep by the cackling of the geese, seized his arms.

17. The first of the Gauls, being thrown down by Manlius, upset those next to him, and the whole line was carried down headlong.

18. When Manlius had been praised for his courage, the sentry, by whose fault the Gauls had climbed up, was hurled down from the rock.

19. Now each army pressed by hunger [hunger pressing] wished for peace.

20. A truce having been made, it was arranged between the leaders on both sides that the Gauls, having received a thousand pounds of gold, should go away from Rome.

21. Some say that the chieftain of the Gauls added his sword to the weight, and exclaimed "Woe to the conquered!"

22. *In the midst of* [*inter*] the bargaining Camillus arrived with his army, and gave orders that the gold should be taken away.

23. He said that Rome must be won back with steel, not gold.

24. Now, fortune being changed, the Romans routed the Gauls at the first onset.

25. Camillus also conquered the Gauls in a second battle, and having taken their camp, returned to Rome in triumph.

ABBREVIATIONS.

a.	=	active.	m.	=	masculine.
abl.	=	ablative.	n.	=	neuter.
acc.	=	accusative.	nom.	=	nominative.
adj.	=	adjective.	part.	=	participle.
adv.	=	adverb.	pass.	=	passive.
comp.	=	comparative.	perf	=	perfect.
conj.	=	conjunction.	pl.	=	plural.
dep.	=	deponent.	prep.	=	preposition.
f.	=	feminine.	pron.	=	pronoun.
gen.	=	genitive.	rel.	=	relative.
gov.	=	governing.	sing.	=	singular.
indecl.	=	indeclinable.	subs.	=	substantive.
impers.	=	impersonal.	superl.	=	superlative.
irreg.	=	irregular.	v.	=	verb.

Note.—Proper names of no importance, or about which the text gives sufficient information, are not included in the Vocabulary.

VOCABULARY.

a, ab, *prep. gov. abl.*, from, by.

abdo, -didi, -ditum, *v. 3 a.*, put away, hide.

abdīco, *v. 1 a., with reflex. pron.* **and** *abl. of thing,* resign.

abdūco, duxi, ductum, *v. 3 a.*, lead away.

abjīcio, -jeci, -jectum, *v. 3 a.*, throw away.

abscēdo, -cessi, -cessum, *v. 3 n.*, go away.

abscīdo, -cīdi, -cīsum, *v. 3 a.*, cut off.

absens, *part. of* absum, absent.

abstergo, -si, -sum, *v. 3 a.*, wipe off.

abstīneo, -tinui, -tentum, *v. 2 a.* **and** *n.*, keep away, abstain.

absum, -esse, -fui, be away, be distant.

ăbundo, *v. 1 n.*, overflow.

ac, atque, *conj.*, and.

accēdo, -cessi, -cessum, *v. 3 n.*, approach, be added.

accendo, -cendi, -censum, *v. 3 a.*, light, set on fire.

accīdo, -cīdi, *v. 3 n.*, befall, happen.

accieo, -ere, *v. 2 a.*, fetch, summon.

accīpio, -cepi, -ceptum, 3 *v. a.*, receive.

ăcerbus, *adj.*, bitter.

ācies, -ei. *subs.* 5, edge, line of battle.

ăd. *prep. gov. acc.*, to, at, near.

addūco, -duxi, -ductum, *v. 3 a.*, lead to, induce.

adeo, -ire, -ivi, or -ii, *v. 4 n.*, approach.

ădeo, *adv.*, so far, to such a degree.

adhortor, *v. 1 dep.*, exhort, encourage.

adīmo, -ēmi, -emptum, *v. 3 a.*, take away.

aditus, -ūs. *subs.* 4, approach.

adjăceo, -jacui, *v. 2 n.*, lie near.

adjīcio, -jeci, -jectum, *v. 3 a.*, add.

adjŭvo, -jūvi, -jūtum, *v. 1 a.*, help.

admīratio, -onis, *subs.* 3 *f.*, wonder, admiration.

admitto, -misi, -missum, v. 3
a., let in; of a horse, to
urge to a gallop.

admŏdum, adv., quite, very.

admŏneo, -ui, -itum, v. 2 a.,
remind, admonish.

admŏveo, -movi, -motum, v.
2, move to, apply.

adŏlescens, part. used as subs.,
young man.

adŏlesco, -evi, v. 2 n., grow
up.

adŏrior, -ortus, v. 4 dep.,
attack.

adsum, -esse, -fui, v.n., be
present.

adsurgo, -surrexi, -surrectum,
v. 3 n., rise up.

advĕho, -vexi, -vectum, v. 3
a., carry to.

advento, v. 1 n., arrive.

adversus, prep. gov. acc., opposite to, against.

adversus, adj., opposite.

advŏco, v. 1 a. call to, summon.

advŏlo, v. 1 n., fly to, hasten
to.

aedes, -is, subs. 3 f., temple,
in pl., house.

aedĭfĭcium, subs. 2 n., building.

aedĭfĭco, v. 1 a., build.

aegre, adv., scarcely, with
difficulty; aegre ferre, to
be displeased at.

Aequi, subs. 2, a tribe south
east of Rome.

aequo, v. 1 a., to equal.

aequus, adj., level, favourable, equal.

aestas, -atis, subs. 3 f., sum-
mer.

aetas, -atis, subs. 3 f., age.

affĕro, -tuli, -latum, v. a.,
bring to, bring news.

affirmo, v. 1 a., assert.

ăger, subs. 2 m., field, land,
territory.

aggrĕdior, -gressus, v. 3 a.,
attack.

ăgĭto, v. 1 a., drive about,
consider.

agmen, -inis, subs. 3 n., army
in line of march, army.

agnosco, -novi, -notum, v. 3
a., recognise, acknowledge.

ăgo, egi, actum, v. 3 a., lead,
drive. Agere cum aliquo,
try to induce any one.

ăgrestis, subs. 3 m., rustic.

Alba, -ae, subs. 1 f., Alba, a
town near Rome.

Albānus, adj., of Alba.

ăla, subs. 1 f., wing.

Algĭdus, subs. 2 m., a mountain near Rome.

ălĭbi, adv., elsewhere. alibi
... alibi, in one place ... in
another.

ălĭēnus, adj., belonging to another, strange, foreign.

ălĭquamdiu, adv., for some
time.

ălĭquantus, adj., somewhat.
-um, subs. n., a consider-
able quantity.

ălĭquotiens, adv., sometimes.

ălĭter, adv., otherwise.

ălius, adj., other.

allŭvies, -ei, subs. f., a pool,
caused by overflow.

ălo, alui, altum, v. 3 a.,
nourish, rear.

alter, adj., the one or the
other of two.

altītūdo, -inis, **subs.** *f.*, height, depth.

altus, *adj.*, high, deep.

alveus, -i, *subs. m.*, tub, river-bed.

ambāges, -is, *subs. f.*, a round-about way. *per ambages*, in mysterious language.

ambītio. **-onis**, *subs. f.*, canvassing for office ; love **of** popularity ; ambition.

ambo, -ae, -o, *adj.*, both.

amitto, -misi, -missum, **v. 3** *a.*, lose.

amŏveo, -mōvi, -mōtum, **v. 2** *a.*, remove.

amplector, -plexus, *v.* 3 *dep.*, embrace.

amplus. *adj.*, large, wide, distinguished.

Amūlius, -i, *subs. m.*, the brother of Numitor, who usurped the throne **of** Alba.

an, conj., *utrum* ... *an*, whether ... or.

anceps, -cipitis, *adj.*, coming from two sides, doubtful.

ănĭmus, **-i**, *subs. m.*, soul, disposition, courage.

Anio, Anienis, *subs. m.*, **a** river running into the Tiber.

annōna, -ae, *subs. f.*, **corn-supply**, price of corn.

anser, -eris, *subs. m.*, goose.

antĕcēdo, **-cessi**, -cessum, **go** before, excel.

antĕquam, *conj.*, before.

Antias, -atis, *adj.*, of **An**-tium.

Antium, -i, *subs.* **n.,** **a** town of Latium.

ăpĕrio, -ui, -apertum, *v.* 4 *a.*, open, disclose.

appāreo, -ui, *v.* 2 *n.*, appear, be evident.

appello, *v.* 1 *a.*, call.

appĕto, -ivi, -itum, *v.* **3** *n.*, approach.

approbo, *v.* 1 *a.*, approve, think well **of**, prove.

apto, *v.* 1 *a.*, fit.

ăpud, *prep. gov.* ***acc.*, at, near.**

ăqua, -ae, *subs. f.*, water.

arceo, -ui, *v.* 2 *a.*, keep off.

arcesso, -ivi, -itum, *v.* 3 *a.*, **send for**, summon.

Ardea, -ae, *subs. f.*, a town **of Latium.**

ardor, -oris, **subs.** *m.*, heat, eagerness.

argūmentum, **-i,** *subs.* **n.,** proof.

arma, -orum, *subs. n.*, arms, armour.

armo, *v.* 1 *a.*, arm.

arx. arcis, *subs. f.*, citadel.

aspernor, *v.* 1 *dep.*, despise.

assĭduus, **adj.**, constant, continual.

atque, *conj.*, and.

atrium, -i, *subs. n.*, hall.

ātrox, **-ocis**, *adj.*, violent, fierce.

attrĭbuo, **-ui**, -utum, *v.* 3 *a.*, assign.

auctor, **-ōris**, *subs. m.*, author, adviser, originator.

audācia, **-ae**, *subs.* ***f.,*** boldness, daring.

audax, -acis, *adj.*, bold.

audeo, ausus, *v.* 2 *semi-dep.*, dare.

audio, *v.* 4 *a.*, hear.

aufŭgio, -fūgi, -fugitum, v. 3
n., flee, take to flight.

augeo, auxi, auctum, v. 2 a.,
increase.

augur, -uris, subs. m., augur,
soothsayer.

augŭrium, -i, subs. n.,
augury, prophecy.

augustus, adj., venerable,
majestic.

aurum, -i, subs. n., gold.

auspĭcium, -i, subs. n., sign,
omen, properly an omen
from flight of birds.

autem, conj., but, and,
now.

auxĭlium, -i, subs. n., help;
auxiliary troops.

Aventinus, -i, subs. m. also
adj., one of the seven hills
of Rome.

āversus, adj., turned away,
having one's back turned.

averto, -verti, -versum, v. 3
a., to turn away.

ăvis, -is, subs. f., bird.

ăvus, -i, subs. m., grand-
father.

barbărus, adj., foreign, bar-
barian.

bellum, -i, subs. n., war.

bĕnĕ, adv., well.

bĕnĕfĭcium, -i, subs. n., a
kindness, benefit.

bĕnigne, adv., favourably.

bĕnignitas, -atis, subs. f.,
kindness, courtesy.

bini, distrib. adj., two each.
with pl. noun, two.

bŏnus, adj., good.

brāchium, -i, subs. n., arm.

brĕvis, -e, adj., short.

brĕvi, abl. of brevis, in a
short time.

cădo, cecidi, casum, v. 3 n.,
fall.

caedes, -is, subs. f., slaughter.

caelestis, -e, adj., of the
heavens. — aqua, rain.

Caere, subs. n. indecl., a town
in Etruria.

calcar, -āris, subs. n., spur.

campus, -i, subs. m., plain.

căno, cecini, cantum, v. 3 n.,
sing, play; prophesy.

Căpēnas, -atis, adj., of
Capena, a city of Etruria.

căpesso, -ivi, -itum, v. 3 a.,
seize.

căpio, cepi, captum, v. 3 a.,
take, capture.

Căpĭtōlium, -i, subs. n., the
Capitol at Rome.

captivus, adj., captured, a
prisoner.

capto, v. 1 a., to endeavour
to catch; to lie in wait for.

căreo, -ui, v. 2 n., to be without.

carmen, -inis, subs. n., song.

Carmentalis, -e, adj. — porta,
a gate of Rome near the
temple of Carmentis.

cāsus, -ūs, subs. m., fall,
chance, accident.

căveo, căvi, cautum, v. 2 n.,
be on one's guard, beware
of.

căvillor, -atus, v. 1 dep., jest,
joke.

cēdo, cessi, cessum, v. 3 n.,
go, yield, give way.

cĕlĕbratus, adj., customary,
brilliant

cĕlĕrĭtas, -ātis, *subs. f.*, swiftness, speed.

censeo, -ui, censum, *v.* 2 *a.*, reckon, esteem, express an opinion.

centŭrio, -ouis, *subs. m.*, centurion.

cerno, crevi, cretum, *v.* 3 *a.*, distinguish, discern, perceive, decide.

certāmen, -inis, *subs. n.*, contest, battle.

certo, *v.* 1 *a.*, strive, contend, fight.

certus, *adj.*, sure, certain, fixed.

cētērus, *adj.*, the rest.

cĭbāria, -orum, *sub. n. pl.*, provisions.

cĭbus, -i, *subs. m.*, food.

cieo, cīvi, cītum, *v.* 2 *a.*, rouse, excite, summon.

Cincinnatus, -i, *subs. m.*, a Roman dictator.

Circeii, -orum, *subs. m.*, a town in Latium.

circum, circa, *prep. gov. acc.*, around, about.

circumāro, *v.* 1 *a.*, to plough round.

circumdo, -dedi, -datum, *v.* 1 *a.*, put round, surround.

circumeo, -ivi, -itum, *v.* 4 *a.*, go round, encompass.

circumfĕro, -tuli, -latum, *v.* 3 *a.*, carry round.

circummitto, -misi, -missum, *v.* 3 *a.*, send round.

circumsĕdeo, -sedi, -sessum, *v.* 2 *a.*, sit round, blockade, besiege.

circumsŏno, -sonui, -sonitum, *v.* 1 *a.* and *n.*, **to** resound on every side.

circumspecto, *v.* 1 *a.*, look round.

circumvallo, *v.* 1 *a.*, to surround with a rampart, blockade.

circumvĕhor, -vectus, *v.* 3 *pass.*, to be carried round, ride round.

circumvĕnio, -veni, -ventum, *v.* 4 *a.*, surround.

cis, citra, *prep. gov. acc.*, on this side.

cĭtatus, *part.*, rapid.

cĭto, *v.* 1 *a.*, to put to quick motion, incite.

cīvīlis, -e, *adj.*, of a citizen, befitting a citizen.

cīvis, -is, *subs. m.* and *f.*, a citizen, a fellow-citizen.

cīvĭtas, -atis, *subs. f.*, citizenship; a state.

clādes, -is, *subs. f.*, disaster, loss.

clāmor, -oris, *subs. m.*, shout, cry.

clangor, -oris, *subs. m.*, clang, noise.

clārus, *adj.*, clear, bright; loud; renowned, famous.

claudo, clausi, clausum, *v.* 3 *a.*, shut.

claustra, -orum, *subs. n. pl.*, a fastening, lock.

Clusinus, *adj.*, of Clusium.

Clusium, -i, *subs. m.*, a town in Etruria.

coăcervo, *v.* 1 *a.*, to heap together.

Cocles, -itis, *subs. m.*, the *cognomen* of Horatius.

coeo, -ivi or -ii, -itum, come together, assemble.

cognitio. -onis, *subs. f.,* knowledge, acquaintance.

cognomen, -inis, *subs. n.,* family name, surname.

cognosco, -gnovi, -gnitum, *v.* 3 *a.,* to find out, learn.

cogo, coegi, coactum, *v.* 3 *a.,* compel.

cohaereo, -haesi, haesum, *v.* 2 *n.,* cling together.

cohors, -hortis, *subs. f.,* cohort, the tenth part of a legion.

colligo, -egi, -ectum, *v.* 3 *a.,* to bring together, collect.

Collinus, *adj.* — *porta,* Colline gate, at Rome.

collis, -is, *subs. m.,* hill.

colloquium, -i, *subs. n.,* conversation.

colo. colui, cultum, *v.* 3 *a.,* cultivate ; honour, revere.

colonia, -ae, *subs. f.,* colony.

colonus, -i, *subs. m.,* farmer, colonist.

cominus, *adv.,* hand to hand, at close quarters.

comitium, -i, *subs. n.,* a place near the forum. where public assemblies were held ; assembly for holding the elections.

comitor, -atus, *v.* 1 *dep.,* accompany.

commendo, *v.* 1 *a.,* intrust, commit.

commeo, *v.* 1 *n.,* to go to and fro.

commoveo, -movi, -motum, *v.* 2 *a.,* move, disturb : rouse, provoke, excite.

communio, -ivi, -itum, *v.* 4 *a.,* to fortify.

comparo, *v.* 1 *a..* get ready, prepare.

compello, -puli, -pulsum, *v.* 3 *a.,* gather together ; compel.

complector. -plexus, *v.* 3 *dep.,* embrace.

complexus, -ûs, *subs. m.,* embrace.

compono, -posui, -positum, put together, arrange.

compositus, *part.,* arranged ; *ex composito,* by arrangement.

comprehendo, -di, -sum, *v.* 3 *a.,* catch hold of, seize.

concedo, -cessi, -cessum, *v.* 3 *a.,* retire ; yield, give up.

concilium, -i, *subs. n.,* assembly.

concito, *v.* 1 *a.,* rouse, excite.

conclamo, *v.* 1 *a.,* cry out together.

concordia, -ae, *subs. f.,* union, concord.

concurro, -curri, -cursum, *v.* 3 *n.,* run together.

concursus, -ûs, *subs. m.,* a running together ; onset, charge.

conditor, -oris, *subs. m.,* founder.

condo, -didi, -ditum, *v.* 3 *a.,* found.

confero, -tuli, -latum, *v.* 3 *a.,* bring together, compare.

confessio. -onis, *subs. f.,* confession.

confestim, *adv.,* immediately.

conficio, -feci, -fectum, *v.* 3 *a.,* finish, complete.

confirmo, *v.* 1 *a.*, strengthen, encourage.

confligo, -flixi, -flictum, *v.* 3 *n.*, dash together, struggle.

confluens, -entis, *subs. m.; also used in pl.*, place where two rivers meet.

confugio, -fūgi, -fugitum, *v.* 3 *n.*, fly for refuge.

congrědior, -gressus, *v.* 3 *dep.*, meet.

congrěgo, *v.* 1 *a.*, collect ; *in pass.* to assemble.

congruo, -ui, *v.* 3 *n.*, agree, coincide.

conjicio, -jeci, -jectum, *v.* 3 *a.*, hurl, throw.

conjūro, *v.* 1 *a.*, swear together, unite, conspire.

conjux, -jugis, *subs. f. and m.*, wife, husband.

conscrībo, -scripsi, -scriptum, *v.* 3 *a.*, to enrol.

conscriptus, *part.* enrolled, elected : used in addressing the Senate.

cŏnor, *v.* 1 *dep.*, try, attempt.

consensus, -us, *subs. m.*, agreement, general consent.

consentio, -sensi, -sensum, *v.* 4 *n.*, agree, consent.

consěro, -serui, -sertum, *v.* 3 *a.*, join ; join battle.

consīdo, -sedi, -sessum, *v.* 3 *a.*, sit down ; encamp.

consīlium, -i, *subs. n.*, deliberation, plan, purpose ; device, stratagem; wisdom.

consisto, -stiti, -stitum, *v.* 3 *n.*, stand still, halt.

consŏcio, *v.* 1 *a.*, share, unite.

conspectus, -us, *subs. m.*, sight.

conspĭcio, -spexi, -spectum, *v.* 3 *a.*, to behold.

conspicor, *v.* 1 *dep.*, catch sight of.

constītuo, -ui, -utum, *v.* 3 *a.*, to station, place ; set up, arrange ; fix, determine.

consto, -stiti, -statum, *v.* 1 *n.*, stand firm ; *impers.*, it is well known.

consuesco, -suevi, -suetum, *v.* 1 *n.*, to grow accustomed.

consul, -ŭlis, *subs. m.*, consul, chief magistrate at Rome.

consŭlaris, -e, *adj.*, of a consul.

consŭlo, -lui, -ltum, *v.* 3 *a.* *and n.*, to consult.

consultum, -i, *subs. n.*, decree.

consūmo, -mpsi, -mptum, *v.* 3 *a.*, to spend, use up, waste.

consurgo, -surrexi, -surrectum, *v.* 3 *n.*, rise up.

contemno, -tempsi, -temptum, *v.* 3 *a.*, despise.

contemplor, *v.* 1 *dep.*, gaze at, observe.

conterreo, -ui, -itum, *v.* 2 *a.*, frighten.

contineo, -ui, -tentum, *v.* 2 *a.*, hold together, check.

contĭnuo, *v.* 1 *a.*, to carry on without interruption.

contĭnuus, *adj.*, unbroken, continuous, successive.

contio, -onis, *subs. f.*, assembly, discourse, speech.

conūbium, -i, *subs. n.*, alliance by marriage, right of intermarriage.

convello, -velli, -vulsum, *v.* 3
a., tear up, pull up.

convĕnio, -veni, -ventum, *v.*
4 *n.*, assemble, meet together ; *impers*, it is agreed
upon.

coorior, -ortus, *v.* 4 *dep.*, arise,
(of war) break out.

cōpia, -ae, *subs. f.*, plenty,
supply ; *in pl.*, forces.

cŏquo, coxi, coctum, *v.* 3 *a.*,
cook.

cōram, *prep. gov. abl. and
adv.*, in presence of, face to
face.

Cŏriŏlanus, -i, *cognomen* of
Cn. Marcius, who took
Corioli.

Cŏriŏli, -orum, *subs. pl. m.*, a
town of the Volscians.

cornu, ūs, *subs. n.*, horn ; the
wing of an army.

corpus, -ŏris, *subs. n.*, body.

cortex, -ĭcis, *subs. m.*, bark,
cork.

crēdo, -didi, -ditum, *v.* 3 *a.*,
entrust ; believe.

Crĕmĕra, -ae, *subs. f.*, a river
in Etruria.

creo, *v.* 1 *a.*, create, appoint.

crĕpĭtus, -ūs, *subs. m.*, ratt-
ling, creaking sound.

cresco, crevi, cretum, *v.* 3
n., grow.

crīnis, -is, *m.*, hair.

cum, *prep. gov. abl.*, with.

cŭmŭlus, -i, *subs. m.*, heap,
pile.

cunctatio, -onis, *subs. f.*, lin-
gering, hesitation, delay.

cunctor, *v.* 1 *dep.*, to delay.

cunctus, *adj.*, all together.

cŭnīculus, -i, *subs. m.*, an
underground passage,
mine.

cŭpīdo, -inis, *subs. f.*, desire.

cūria, -ae, *subs. f.*, senate-
house.

Curiatii, *subs. m.*, an Alban
family, three of whom
fought against the Horatii.

cūro, *v.* 1 *a.*, take care of,
look after.

currus, -ūs, *subs. m.*, chariot,
car.

cursus, ūs, *subs. m.*, running,
course.

cŭrulīs, *adj.* — *sella*, curule
chair, used by consuls,
praetors, aediles, etc.

cuspis, -idis, *subs. f.*, point,
spike ; spear, javelin.

custōdia, -ae, *subs. f.*, guard,
watching, care.

custos, ŏdis, *subs. m.*, a guard,
watchman, keeper.

damno, *v.* 1 *a.*, condemn.

dē, *prep. gov. abl.*, down from,
from, concerning.

dĕcem, *adj. indecl.*, ten.

dĕcerno, -crevi, -cretum, *v.* 3
a., to decide, decree, or-
dain.

dĕcĭmus, *adj.*, tenth.

decĭpio, -cepi, -ceptum, *v.* 3
a., deceive.

decrētum, -i, *subs. n.*, decree.

decurro, -curri, -cursum, *v.* 3
n., run down.

dĕcus, -oris, *subs. n.*, grace,
ornament, pride, glory.

dedĭcatio, -onis, *subs. f.*, dedi-
cation.

dedĭco, *v.* 1 *a.*, dedicate.

deditio, -ouis, *subs. f.*, surrender.

dedo, -didi, -ditum, *v.* 3 *a.*, to surrender.

deduco, -duxi, -ductum, *v.* 3 *a.*, lead down, lead forth.

defendo, -di, -sum, *v.* 3 *a.*, ward off, defend.

defero, -tuli, -latum, *v.* 3 *a.*, carry down, bring news, give information.

deficio, -feci, -fectum, *v.* 3 *a.*, desert, revolt from.

defigo, -fixi, -fixum, *v.* 3 *a.*, fasten down, fix.

defluo, -fluxi, -fluxum, *v.* 3 *n.*, flow down.

defodio, -fodi, -fossum, *v.* 3 *a.*, dig down, bury in the ground.

defugio, -fugi, -fugitum, *v.* 3 *a.*, run away from, avoid.

defungor, -functus, *v.* 3 *dep.*, perform.

degredior, -gressus, *v.* 3 *dep.*, march down, descend.

dein, deinde, *adv.*, thence, afterwards.

dejicio, -jeci, -jectum, *v.* 3 *a.*, throw down.

delectus, ûs, *subs. m.*, a choosing, a levy of troops.

deleo, -levi, -letum, *v.* 2 *a.*, blot out, destroy utterly.

deligo, -legi, -lectum, *v.* 3 *a.*, pick out, choose.

Delphi, -orum, *subs. m.*, a town in Greece famed for its oracle of Apollo.

Delphicus, *adj.*, of Delphi.

demigro, *v.* 1 *a.*, depart, emigrate.

demum, *adv.*, at length.

denuntio, *v.* 1 *a.*, give notice, declare, threaten.

depello, -puli, -pulsum, *v.* 3 *a.*, drive away.

deprehendo, -di, -sum, *v.* 3 *a.*, to seize, overtake, catch.

descendo, -di, -sum, *v.* 3 *a.*, come down, descend.

desero, -ui, -tum, *v.* 3 *a.*, desert.

desiderium, -i, *subs. n.*, longing, regret for something lost.

desilio, -ui, -sultum, *v.* 4 *n.*, leap down.

despero, *v.* 1 *a.*, despair.

destino, *v.* 1 *a.*, to design, intend, appoint.

destituo, -ui, -utum, *v.* 3 *a.*, forsake, abandon, defraud.

deterreo, -ui, -itum, *v.* 2 *a.*, frighten from, deter.

detraho, -traxi, -tractum, *v.* 3 *a.*, drag off, deprive.

detrecto, *v.* 1 *a.*, draw back from, decline.

detrudo, -trusi, -trusum, *v.* 3 *a.*, thrust down.

deturbo, *v.* 1 *a.*, cast down, dislodge, dash to the ground.

deus, -i, *subs. m.*, god.

dexter, -tra, -trum, *or* -tera, -terum, *adj.*, to the right. *dextra*, *dextera*, the right hand.

dico, -xi, -ctum, *v.* 3 *a.*, say, name.

dictator, -oris, *subs. m.*, dictator, a supreme magistrate appointed at Rome in times of special danger.

dīdūco, -xi, -ctum, *v.* 3 *a.*, draw apart, disperse.

dies, -ei. *subs. m. sometimes f. in sing.*, day.

dignus, *adj.*, worthy.

dīlābor, -lapsus, *r.* 3 *dep.*, fall asunder, disperse.

dīmĭcātio, -onis, *subs. f.*, fight, combat.

dīmĭco, *v.* 1 *a.*, to fight a battle.

dīmitto, -misi, -missum, *v.* 3 *a.*, send away.

dīrĭgo, -rexi, -rectum, *v.* 3 *a.*, set straight, draw up in a straight line.

dirĭmo, -emi, -emptum, *v.* 3 *a.*, separate, part.

dirĭpio, -ui, -reptum, *v.* 3 *a.*, tear in pieces, plunder, ravage.

discēdo, -cessi, -cessum, *v.* 3 *a.*, depart.

discerno, -crevi, -cretum, *v.* 3 *a.*, separate, discern.

disciplina, -ae, *subs. f.*, teaching, training.

discordia, -ae. *subs. f.*, disagreement, dissension.

discrimen, -inis, *subs. m.*, distance, distinction. critical moment, risk, crisis.

discurro, -curri, -cursum, *v.* 3 *n.*, run in different directions.

dispar, *adj.*, unequal.

dispōno, -posui, -positum, *v.* 3 *a.*, arrange.

dissĭmŭlo, *v.* 1 *a.*, to pretend that a thing is not, disguise, conceal.

dissĭpo, *v.* 1 *a.*, scatter, disperse.

dissŏnus, *adj.*, discordant.

distĭneo, -ui, -tentum, *r.* 2 *a.*, keep apart.

disto, *no perf. or sup.*, *v.* 1 *n.*, to stand apart.

dīvĭdo, -si, -sum, *v.* 1 *a.*, divide.

do, dedi, datum, *v.* 1 *a.*, give.

dŏceo, -ui, doctum, *r.* 2 *a.*, teach.

dŏlor, -oris, *subs. m.*, pain.

dŏlus, -i, *subs. m.*, deceit, stratagem.

dŏmo, -ui, -itum, *v.* 1 *a.*, tame, subdue.

dŏmus, -ūs, *subs. f.* 2 *and* 4, house.

dōnec, *conj.*, while, until.

dōnum, -i, *subs. m.*, gift.

dŭbius, *adj.*, doubtful, uncertain.

dūco, -xi, -ctum, *r.* 3 *a.*, lead, consider.

ductus, -us, *subs. m.*, leadership.

dulcēdo, -inis, *subs. f.*, sweetness, charm.

dum, *conj.*, whilst, until, provided that.

duo, -ae, -o, *num. adj.*, two.

dŭŏdēni, *distrib. adj.*, twelve each.

dŭplex, -icis, *adj.*, twofold, double.

dux, dŭcis, *subs. m.*, leader, guide, general.

ē, ex, *prep. gov. abl.*, out of, from.

ĕburneus, *adj.*, of ivory.

edīco, -xi, -ctum, *v.* 3 *a.*, proclaim.

edictum, -i, *subs. n.*, proclamation.

editus, *part.*, elevated, lofty.

ēdo, -didi, -ditum, *v.* 3 *a.*, give forth, give birth to, utter, proclaim.

edūco, *v.* 1 *a.*, bring up, educate.

edūco, -xi, -ctum, *v.* 3 *a.*, lead out.

effūgio, -fūgi, -fūgitum, *v.* 3 *a.*, escape.

effundo, -fudi, -fusum, *v.* 3 *a.*, pour out.

ēgeo, -ui, *v.* 2 *n.*, suffer want, be in need of.

egrēdior, -gressus, *v.* 3 *dep.*, march out, go out.

egrēgius, *adj.*, uncommon, distinguished, brilliant.

elīcio, -licui *or* lexi, -licitum, *v.* 3 *a.*, entice out, draw out.

elūdo, -lusi, -lusum, *v.* 3 *a.*, baffle, deceive.

emitto, -misi, -missum, *v.* 3 *a.*, send out, let out.

enītor, -nisus *or* -nixus, *v.* 3 *dep.*, climb, strive, struggle.

eo, ivi, itum, *v.* 4 *n.*, go.

ĕpūlae, -arum, *subs. f. pl.*, feast, banquet.

ĕpūlor, *v.* 1 *dep.*, to feast.

ĕques, -itis, *subs. m.*, horseman, knight.

ĕquitātūs, -ūs, *subs. m.*, cavalry.

ĕquus, -i, *subs. m.*, horse.

erga, *prep. gov. acc.*, towards.

ergo, *adv.*, consequently, therefore, on account of.

erīpio, -ui, -reptum, *v.* 3 *a.*, snatch out, rescue.

erumpo, -rupi, -ruptum, *v.* 3 *n.*, burst forth.

et, *conj.*, and, also. et ... et, both ... and.

Etruria, -ae, *subs. f.*, a district of Italy north of the Tiber.

Etruscus, *adj.*, of Etruria, Etruscan.

etsi, *conj.*, although.

evādo, -vasi, -vasum, *v.* 3 *n.*, go out, turn out; escape.

evēho, -vexi, -vectum, *v.* 3 *a.*, carry out.

exaudio, *v.* 4 *a.*, overhear.

excēdo, -cessi, -cessum, *v.* 3 *n.*, go out, depart.

excīdium, -i, *subs. n.*, overthrow, destruction.

excieo *or* -cio, -civi, -citum, *v.* 2. *a.*, bring out, rouse, excite.

excīpio, -cepi, -ceptum, *v.* 3 *a.*, take out, except.

exercītus, -us, *subs. m.*, army.

exhaurio, -hausi, -haustum, *v.* 4 *a.*, draw out, empty, exhaust.

exĭguus, *adj.*, scanty, small, mean.

exīlium, -i, *subs. n.*, exile.

exīmius, *adj.*, distinguished, excellent.

exīmo, -emi, -emptum, *v.* 3 *a.*, take out, release.

exītus, -ūs, *subs. m.*, departure, way out, issue, result.

expecto, *v.* 1 *a.*, to await.

expēdio, *v.* 4 *a.*, set free, extricate ; disclose.

expello, -puli, -pulsum, v. 3 a., drive out.

expiro, v. 1 a. and n., breathe out, expire.

expleo, -plevi, -pletum, v. 2 a., fill up, complete.

expono, -posui, -positum, v. 3 a., put out, expose; set forth, explain.

exprimo, -pressi, -pressum, v. 3 a., squeeze out, extort, express.

expugno, v. 1 a., take by storm.

exsanguis, -e, adj., bloodless.

exsequor, -secutus, v. 3 dep., follow out, pursue; carry out: describe fully.

exsto, v. 1 n., stand out, be visible.

exta, -orum, subs. n., entrails.

extemplo, adv., immediately.

externus, adj., from outside.

exterreo, v. 2 a., frighten.

exterus, adj., outside, foreign.

extinguo, -nxi, -nctum, v. 3 a., put out, quench, destroy.

extorqueo, -torsi, -tortum, v. 2 a., wrench away, take by force.

extra, adv. and prep. gor. acc., outside, beyond.

extrinsecus, adv., from outside.

exul, -ulis, subs. m., exile.

exulo, v. 1 n., to live in exile.

exulto, v. 1 a., to exult, rejoice.

exuo, -ui, -utum, v. 3 a., strip, deprive.

Fabius, subs. m., and adj., the name of a gens, or clan, at Rome.

fabula, -ae, subs. f., a story.

facinus, -oris, subs. m., a deed, esp. daring deed; crime.

facio, feci, factum, v. 3, do, make.

factum, -i, subs. n., deed.

Falerii, -orum, subs. m., a city of Etruria.

Faliscus, adj., of Falerii: the Falisci.

fallo, fefelli, falsum, v. 3 a., to deceive, escape notice of.

fama, -ae, subs. f., report, rumour.

fames, -is, subs. f., hunger, famine.

familia, -ae, subs. f., family.

familiaris, -e, adj., pertaining to the family, familiar; as subs., a familiar friend.

fatalis, -e, adj., destined by fate.

fatum, -i, subs. n., fate, destiny.

Faustulus, -i, subs. m., the shepherd who brought up Romulus and Remus.

faustus, adj., favourable, fortunate.

felix, adj., lucky, successful.

ferus, adj., wild; fera, subs., wild beast.

Feretrius, subs., a surname of Jupiter.

ferme, adv., nearly, about.

fero, tuli, latum, v. 3 a., to bear, carry, report.

ferox, adj., daring, warlike.

ferrum, -i, *subs.*, iron, steel ; the sword.

fessus, *adv.*, weary.

festīno, *v.* 1 *a. and n.*, to hasten, hurry.

Fīdēnae, -arum, *subs. f.*, a Sabine town five miles north-east of Rome.

Fidenas, -atis, *adj.*, of Fidenae ; *in pl.*, the people of F.

fīdo, fisus, *v.* 3 *semi-dep.*, to trust.

fīdus, *adj.*, trusty, firm, sure.

fīgo, fixi, fixum, *v.* 3 *a.*, to fix, fasten.

fīlius, -i, *subs. m.*, son.

fīnis, -is, *subs. m.*, boundary, limit, end; *in pl.*, territory.

fīnītīmus, *adj.*, bordering on, neighbouring ; *in pl. as subs.*, neighbours.

fīo, factus, *v. irreg.*, become, be made.

firmo, *v.* 1 *a.*, strengthen.

firmus, *adj.*, strong.

flāgro, *v.* 1 *a.*, to blaze.

flāmen, -inis, *subs. m.*, priest.

flecto, flexi, flexum, *v.* 3 *a.*, bend, turn.

flētus, -us, *subs. m.*, weeping.

fluīto, *v.* 1 *a.*, to float, drift.

flūmen, -inis, *subs. m.*, river.

fluo, fluxi, -xum, *v.* 3 *n.*, flow.

fōculus, -i, *subs. m.*, a little hearth, brazier.

foedus, -eris, *subs. n.*, treaty, agreement.

fors, fortis, *subs. f.*, chance.

forte, *adv.*, by chance (*abl.* of *fors*).

fortis, -e, *adj.*, strong, brave.

fortitudo, -inis, *subs. f.*, courage, resolution.

fortuna, -ae, *subs. f.*, chance, fortune.

fŏrum, -i, *subs. n.*, market-place.

fossa, -ae, *subs. f.*, ditch, trench.

frăgor, -oris, *subs. m.*, crash.

frango, fregi, fractum, *v.* 3 *a.*, break.

frāter, -tris, *subs. m.*, brother.

fraus, fraudis, *subs. f.*, deceit, treachery, trick.

frĕquens, *adj.*, frequent, crowded, frequented.

frūgem, -is, *pl.*, fruges, frugum, *no nom. sing. in use*, *subs. f.*, fruits of the earth.

frūmentum, -i, *subs. n.*, corn.

fruor, fruitus *and* fructus, *v.* 3 *n.*, enjoy.

frustror, *v.* 1 *dep.*, deceive, disappoint.

fūga, -ae, *subs. f.*, flight.

fŭgo, *v.* 1 *a.*, to put to flight.

fundo, fudi, fusum, *v.* 3 *a.*, to pour out, to rout the enemy.

Gābīnus, *adj.*, of Gabii, a town in Latium.

gaudeo, gavisus, *v.* 2 *semi-dep.*, rejoice.

gaudium, -i, *subs. n.*, joy.

gĕmĭno, *v.* 1 *a.*, to double.

gĕminus, *adj.*, twin ; double.

gĕner, -eri, *subs. m.*, son-in-law.

gens, -tis, *subs. f.*, clan, family ; race, nation.

gĕro, gessi, gestum, *v.* 3 *a.*, bear, carry, carry on, wage (war).

gigno, genui, genitum, *v.* 3 *a.*, bring forth, produce.

glădius, -i, *subs. m.*, sword.

glōria, -ae, *subs. f.*, glory.

grassor, *v.* 1 *dep.*, walk about, prowl, advance, proceed.

grātes, *f. pl.*, thanks.

grātia, -ae, *subs. f.*, favour, thanks, gratitude.

grātulor, *v.* 1 *dep.*, congratulate.

grātus, *adj.*, pleasing, acceptable; thankful.

grăvis, -e, *adj.*, heavy, serious, important.

grăvitas, -atis, *subs. f.*, weight, dignity.

gurges, -itis, *subs. m.*, abyss, flood, eddy.

hăbeo, *v.* 2 *a.*, have.

haereo, haesi, haesum, *v.* 3 *n.*, to stick, cling; hesitate.

hăruspex, -icis, *subs. m.*, soothsayer.

hasta, -ae, *subs. f.*, spear.

haud, *adv.*, not.

haurio, hausi, haustum, *v.* 4 *a.*, draw up, drink in, drain, empty.

Herminius, T., one of the companions of Horatius on the bridge, afterwards killed at Lake Regillus.

Hernīci, -orum, a people of Latium.

hībernāculum, -i, *subs. n. in. pl.*, winter-quarters.

hic, *pron.*, this, he.

hiccine, = hic, with interrogative particle.

hiemo, *v.* 1 *n.*, to spend the winter, to keep in winter-quarters.

hiems, -emis, *subs. f.*, winter.

hinc, *adv.*, hence.

hŏnor, -is, *subs. m.*, public honour, office.

hŏnōro, *v.* 1 *a.*, to honour.

Hŏratius, name of a Roman *gens*, or clan.

horrendus, *part.*, dreadful, terrible.

hospĭtium, -i, *subs. n.*, hospitality.

hostia, -ae, *subs. f.*, victim.

hostilis, -e, *adj.*, hostile.

hostis, -is, *subs. n.*, enemy.

hŭmanus, *adj.*, human, befitting a man.

hŭmilitas, -ātis, *subs. f.*, lowness, humble condition.

hŭmus, -i, *subs. f.*, earth, ground.

hŭmi, *adv.*, (really locative case of *humus*), on the ground.

ĭbi, *adv.*, there.

īco, ici, ictum, *v.* 3 *a.*, to strike.

ĭgĭtur, *adv.*, therefore.

ignis, -is, *subs. m.*, fire.

ignārus, *adj.*, ignorant.

ignōro, *v.* 1 *a.*, to be ignorant.

ille, *pron.*, that, he, she, it.

immensus, *adj.*, not measured, immense.

immĭneo, -ni, -utum, *v.* 2 *n.*, to overhang, to be near to.

immŏlo, *v.* 1 *a.*, to sacrifice.

immortalis, -e, *adj.*, immortal.

impar, *adj.*, unequal.

impĕdio, *v.* 4 *a.*, to hinder.
impello, -pŭli, -pulsum, *v.* 3
a., to urge on.
impĕrātor, -oris, *subs. m.*,
commander-in-chief.
impĕrīto, *v.* 1 *a.*, to command,
govern.
impĕrītus, *adj.*, unskilled,
gov. gen.
impĕrium, -i, *subs. n.*, autho-
rity, command.
impĕro, *v.* 1 *a.*, to command,
order, demand.
impĕtro, *v.* 1 *a.*, to obtain (by
asking).
impĕtus, -ūs, *subs. m.*, attack,
assault, rush.
impĭger, -gra, -grum, *adj.*,
energetic, active.
impĭgre, *adv.*, actively,
readily.
impleo, -plevi, -pletum, *v.* 2
a., fill up.
implŏro, *v.* 1 *a.*, to invoke,
beseech.
impŏtens, *adj.*, feeble ; not
master of oueself, ungovern-
able.
imprŏvĭdus, *adj.*, not fore-
seeing, improvident.
in, *prep. gov. acc.*, into, to,
against. *gov. abl.*, in, on.
incassum, *adv.*, in vain.
incēdo, -cessi, -cessum, *v.* 3
a., march along, advance.
incendium, -i, *subs. n.*, fire,
conflagration.
incertus, *adj.*, uncertain.
incĭdo, -cidi, -casum, *v.* 3 *n.*,
fall upon, fall in with, fall
into.
incĭpio, -cepi, -ceptum, *v.* 3 *a.*,
begin.

inclāmo, *v.* 1 *a.*, invoke, call
out to.
inclīno, *v.* 1 *a.* and *n.*, bend
down, give way.
incŏlŭmis, -e, *adj.*, unhurt,
safe, sound.
incondĭtus, *adj.*, confused,
rude.
incrĕpo, -ui, -itum, *v.* 1 *a.*, re-
proach, rebuke.
incruentus, *adj.*, bloodless.
incŭbo, -ui, -itum, *v.* 1 *n.*, lie
upon, lean upon.
incursĭo, -onis, *subs. f.*, raid,
assault.
incurso, *v.* 1 *a.*, to assault,
make a raid upon.
inde, *adv.*, thence, after that,
then.
indīco, -dixi, -dictum, *v.* 3 *a.*,
declare, proclaim.
indies, *adv.*, from day to day,
daily.
indignātio, -onis, *subs. f.*, in-
dignation.
indignĭtas, -atis, *subs. f.*, insult.
indignus, *adj.*, unworthy.
ineo, -ivi *or* -ii, -itum, *v.* 4 *a.*,
enter.
inermis, -e, *adj.*, unarmed.
infandus, *adj.*, unspeakable,
abominable.
infans, -ntis, *subs. c.*, child,
infant.
infēlix, *adj.*, unlucky, unfor-
tunate.
infensus, *adj.*, hostile.
infĕro, -tuli, -latum, *v.* 3 *a.*,
bring in, introduce.
infestus, *adj.*, dangerous,
hostile.

infīmus, *adj. superl.*, *from* infra, lowest.

infirmus, *adj.*, feeble.

ingens, *adj.*, huge.

ingrātus, *adj.*, unpleasing, ungrateful.

ingredior, -gressus, *v. 3 dep.*, enter.

initium, -i, *subs. n.*, beginning.

injicio, -jeci, -jectum, *v. 3 a.*, throw in; bring into, cause.

injūria, -ae, *subs.*, wrong.

injussus, *subs. m. used only in abl.*, without the orders of.

innītor, -nisus or -nixus, *v. 3 n.*, rest on, lean on.

inōpia, -ae, *subs. f.*, want, scarcity.

inōpinatūs, *adj.*, unexpected.

inquam, *v. def.*, I say.

insero, -ui, -tum, *v. 3 a.*, bring into, insert.

insīdiae, -arum, *subs. f. pl.*, ambush, artifice.

insignis, -e, *adj.*, conspicuous, distinguished.

insōlens, *adj.*, insolent.

insōlītus, *adj.*, unwonted, unusual.

inspērātus, *adj.*, unhoped for.

instinguo, -nxi, -nctum, *v. 3 a.*, incite, impel, inspire.

insto, -stiti, *v. 1 n.*, stand, approach, impend, press closely on.

instruo, -xi, -ctum, *v. 3 a.*, to build; set in order, draw up (an army).

intactus, *adj.*, untouched.

intĕger, -gra, -grum, *adj.*, untouched, unhurt, whole.

intendo, -di, -tum *and* -sum, *v. 3 a.*, stretch towards, intend.

intentus, *part.*, intent upon.

inter, *prep. gov. acc.*, between, among.

intercurro, -curri, -cursum, *v. 3 n.*, run between; hasten in the meantime.

interficio, -feci, -fectum, *v. 3 a.*, kill.

intĕrim, *adv.*, in the mean time.

intĕrĭmo, -emi, -emptum, *v. 3 a.*, destroy, kill.

intĕrior, *adj. comp.*, *from* intra, inner.

intermitto, -misi, -missum, *v. 3 a.*, to let go between, interrupt.

interpōno, -posui, -positum, *v. 3 a.*, put between.

interpres, -pretis, *subs. c.*, interpreter.

interrumpo, -rupi, -ruptum, *v. 3 a.*, break asunder, break off.

intervallum, -i, *subs. n.*, interval.

intervĕnio, -veni, -ventum, *v. 3 n.*, to come between.

intŏlĕrandus, *adj.*, unbearable.

intra, *adv. and prep. gov. acc.*, within, inside of.

intro, *v. 1 a.*, to enter.

intueor, -itus, *v. 2 dep.*, gaze upon, observe.

intūtūs, *adj.*, defenceless.

invādo, -si, -sum, *v. 3 a.*, enter, assail.

invĕho, -vexi, -vectum, v. 3
a., to carry in. in pass.,
to ride into.

invĕnio, -vēni, -ventum, v. 3
a., to come upon, find.

inviŏlatus, adj., unharmed.

invīsĭtatus, adj., unseen, un-
familiar.

invŏco, v. 1 a., to call upon,
invoke.

ipse, -a, -um, pron., self.

īra, -ae, subs. f., anger.

īrascor, iratus, v. 3 dep., to
grow angry.

irrēlĭgiosus, adj., impious.

irrumpo, -rupi, -ruptum, v. 3
a., to break in.

irruo, -ui, v. 3 a., to rush
into, rush against.

is, ea, id, pron., he, she, it.

īta, adv., thus, so.

īter, itineris, subs. n., jour-
ney, march.

jăceo, -ui, -ctum, v. 2 n., to
lie.

jăcio, jēci, jactum, v. 3 a., to
throw, lay.

jacto, v. 1 a., to throw, toss
about, boast.

jactura, -ae, subs. f., loss.

jam, adv., now.

Jānĭcŭlum, -i, subs. n., one of
the hills of Rome north of
the Tiber.

Jānus, -i, subs., the god
Janus.

jŭbeo, jussi, jussum, v. 3 a.,
to bid, order.

jŭgĕrum, -i, subs. n., a
measure of land, about
two thirds of an acre, in
pl. like 3rd decl.

jŭgŭlum, -i, subs. n., throat.

jŭgum, -i, subs. n., yoke.

jungo, junxi, -nctum, v. 3 a.,
to join, yoke, harness.

Juno, -onis, subs. f., the
queen of the Gods.

Jŭpiter, Jovis, subs. m., king
of the Gods.

jūs, juris, subs. n., right,
law.

jussus, -ūs, subs. m., only in
abl. sing., command.

justītium, -i, subs. n., a cessa-
tion of business.

justus, adj., just, fair,
proper, regular.

jŭvĕnis, adj. and subs.,
young, a youth.

jŭventūs, -utis, subs. f., the
season of youth ; as collect.
subs., the youth.

jŭvo, jūvi, jūtum, v. 1 a., to
help.

lăcus, -ūs, subs. m., lake.

lăcrĭma, -ae, subs. f., tear.

laetĭtia, -ae, subs. f., joy.

lāmentum, -i, subs. n., weeping, lamentation.

lăpis, -idis, subs. m., stone.

Lārentia, -ae, subs. f., wife of
Faustulus, who brought up
Romulus and Remus.

Lătīnus, adj., of Latium,
Latin.

lătro, -onis, subs. m., robber,
brigand.

latrocinium, -i, subs. n., rob-
bery, brigandage.

lătus, -eris, subs. n., side.

laus, laudis, subs. f., praise.

lēgātio, -onis, subs. f., em-
bassy.

lēgātus, -i, *subs. m.*, ambassador, envoy ; lieutenant.

lĕgio. -onis, *subs. f.*, a legion.

lēgo, *v.* 1 *a.*, to send as ambassador ; to leave by will.

lĕgo, lēgi, lectum, *v.* 3 *a.*, to gather, pick, choose out; read.

lēnĭter, *adv.*, gently.

lētum, -i, *subs. n.*, death.

lēvis, -e, *adj.*, light, slight.

līber. -a, -um, *adj.*, free.

līberi, -orum, *subs. m. pl.*, children.

lĭcet, licuit, *v.* 2 *impers.*, it is lawful, it is permitted.

lictor, -oris, *subs. n.*, lictor, an attendant on Roman magistrates.

līmen. -inis, *subs. m.*, threshold, entrance.

lītĕra or littera, -ae, *subs. f.*, a letter of the alphabet ; *in pl.*, a letter, despatch.

lŏco, *v.* 1 *a.*, to place.

lŏcus, -i, *subs. m. pl. -i. and a.*, place.

longe, *adv.*, far, at a distance.

longinquus, *adj.*, remote, distant.

lŏquor, locutus, *v.* 3 *dep.*, to speak.

luctus, -ūs, *subs. m.*, mourning, grief.

lūdĭbrium, -i, *subs. n.*, mockery ; a laughing-stock.

lūdicrum. -i, *subs. n.*, a stage-play.

lūdus, -i, *subs. m.*, game.

lux, lūcis, *subs. f.*, light.

macto, *v.* 1 *a.*, to sacrifice.

maestus, *adj.*, sad.

măgis, *adv.*, more.

măgister, -tri, *subs. m.*, teacher, master.

magnus, *adj.*, great.

mājestas, -atis, *subs. f.*, dignity, majesty.

mălĕ, *adv.*, badly.

mālo, malui, *v. irreg.*, to prefer.

Mămĭlius, -i, *subs. m.*, a chieftain of Tusculum.

mamma, -ae, breast, teat.

mandātum, -i, *subs. n.*, a commission, message.

măneo, mansi, mansum, *v.* 2 *n.*, to remain.

mānes, -ium, *subs. m. pl.*, the spirits of the dead.

māno, *v.* 1 *n.*, to trickle, drop, flow.

mănus, -us, *subs. f.*, hand, band of men.

Marcius, Cn., Roman general, better known as Coriolanus.

Mars, Martis, *subs. m.*, the god of war ; war.

Martius, *adj.*, of Mars, warlike.

matrona, -ae, *subs. f.*, matron.

mātūrus, *adj.*, ripe, fit, reasonable.

Mātūta, -ae. *subs. f.*, the goddess of dawn.

maxĭme, *adv.*, especially, chiefly.

mĕdius, *adj.*, middle.

mĕmĭni, *v. def.*, 1 remember.

mĕmor, -oris, *adj.*, mindful, remembering.

mĕmōria, *subs. f.*, memory.

mens, -ntis, *subs. f.*, mind.

mensis, -is, *subs. m.*, month.
merces, -cēdis, *subs. f.*, pay, reward.
mĕtuo, -ui, *v. 3 a.*, to fear.
mĕtus, -us, *subs. m.*, fear.
mīles, -itis, *subs. m.*, soldier.
milĭtaris, -e, *adj.*, of a soldier, military.
mīlĭtia, -ae, *subs. f.*, military service, warfare.
milĭtor, *v.* **1** *dep.*, to serve as a soldier.
mille, *adj. indecl.*, a thousand.
minae, -arum, *sub. f. pl.*, threats.
mīnor, *v.* **1** *dep.*, to threaten.
mĭnor, -oris, *adj. comp. of parvus*, smaller, less.
mīrăculum, -i, *subs. n.*, miracle.
mīror, *v.* **1** *dep.*, to wonder.
misceo, miscui, **mistum,** *or* mixtum, *v.* **2** *a.*, to mix.
missīlis, -e, *adj.*, that may be thrown, that is thrown.
mitto, misi, missum, *v.* **3** *a.*, to send.
mŏdĭcus, *adj.*, moderate.
mŏdo, *adv.*, only.
mŏdus, -i, *subs. m.*, measure, limit, manner.
moenia, -ium, *subs. n. pl.*, city walls.
mollio, *v.* **4** *a.*, to soften.
mŏmentum, -i, *subs. n.*, movement, short space, cause, impulse.
mons, -ntis, *subs. m.*, mountain.
monstro, *v.* **1** *a.*, to point out, show.
mŏrĭbundus, *adj.*, on the point of death.

mortālis, *adj.*, liable to death, mortal.
mŏveo, mōvi, mōtum, *v.* **2** *a.*, to move.
mox, *adv.*, presently.
Mūcius C., a young Roman who tried to kill Porsena.
mūcro, -onis, *subs. m.*, sharp point, sword.
mŭlĭēbris, -e, *adj.*, womanly.
multĭtudo, -inis, *subs. f.*, multitude.
multus, *adj.*, much, many.
mūnio, *v.* **4** *a.*, to fortify.
mūnītio, -onis, *subs. f.*, fortification.
mūnītor, -oris, *subs. m.*, fortifier, workmen.
mūrus, -i, *subs. m.*, wall.

nam, *conj.*, for.
nanciscor, nactus, *v.* **3** *dep.*, to obtain.
nascor, nātus, *v.* **3** *dep.*, to be born.
nātus, -us, *subs. m.*, birth.
nāvis, -is, *subs. f.*, ship, boat.
nē, *conj.*, that not : *adv.* used with *quidem*, not even.
nec, neque, *conj.*, neither, nor.
nĕcessitas, -atis, *subs. f.*, necessity.
necto, nexui *and* -xi, -xum, *v.* **3** *a.*, to bind, fasten.
nĕfandus, *adj.*, unspeakable, abominable.
neglĭgo, -lexi, -lectum, *v.* **3** *a.*, to neglect, disregard.
nĕgo, *v.* **1** *a.*, to deny.
nēmo, -inis, *subs. m. and f.*, no one (*gen. and abl. not used, supplied from nullus*).

nĕmus, -oris, *subs. n.*, a grove, wood.

nĕpos, -otis, *subs. m.*, guardian.

Neptūnus, -i, *subs. m.*, the god of the sea.

nĕqueo, -ivi *and* -ii, to be unable.

nĭhil, *subs. indec.*, nothing.

nĭhĭli, *adv. (locative case of nihilum)*, at nothing, of no value.

nĭhĭlōminus, *adv.*, none the less.

nĭmis, *adv.*, too much.

nĭsi, *conj.*, unless.

nītor, nisus *or* nixus, *v. 3 dep.*, to lean on, press forward, strive.

no, *v. 1 n.*, to swim.

nōbĭlis, -e, *adj.*, famous, noble.

nōlo, nolui, *v. irreg.*, to be unwilling.

nōmen, -inis, *subs. n.*, name.

non, *adv.*, not.

noscĭto, *v. 1 a.*, to know, recognise.

nōtĭtĭa, -ae, *subs. f.*, acquaintance, knowledge.

nŏvus, *adj.*, new, fresh.

noxa, -ae, *subs. f.*, harm, hurt.

nūdus, *adj.*, naked, exposed.

nŭmᵉro, *v. 1 a.*, to count.

nŭmĕrus, -i, *subs. m.*, number.

Nŭmĭtor, -oris, king of Alba, deposed by his brother Amulius.

nunc, *adv.*, now.

nunquam, *adv.*, never.

nuntio, *v. 1 a.*, to announce, bring news.

nuntĭus, -i, *subs. m.*, messenger, message, news.

nŭrus, -ūs, *subs. f.*, daughter-in-law.

nusquam, *adv.*, nowhere.

ob, *prep. gov. acc.*, on account of.

ŏbeo, -ii *and* -ivi, *v. 4 n.*, to encounter, die.

objĭcio, -jeci, -jectum, *v. 3 a.*, to throw in the way, to expose.

oblīvio, -onis, *subs. f.*, forgetfulness.

obruo, -ui, -utum, *v. 3 a.*, to cover, bury, overwhelm.

obsĕro, -sevi, -situm, *v. 3 a.*, to plant, cover with; *obsitus*, overgrown.

obsĭdeo, -sēdi, -sessum, *v. 2 a.*, to blockade, besiege.

obsĭdio, -onis, *subs. f.*, a blockade, siege.

obstĭnātus, *adj.*, fixed, resolved.

obsto, -stiti, -stitum, *v. 1 n.*, to stand in the way of, hinder, oppose.

obstŭpĕfacio, -feci, -factum, *v. 3 a.*, to astonish, amaze.

obtestor, *v. 1 dep.*, to call as a witness, protest, entreat.

obtĭneo, -ui, -tentum, *v. 2 a.*, to hold, keep possession of.

obtrunco, *v. 1 a.*, to cut down, kill.

obviam, *adv.*, in the way; *obviam ire*, to meet.

occāsus, -ūs, *subs. f.*, setting, downfall.

occīdio, -onis, *subs. f.*, destruction, extermination.

occīdo, -cidi, -cisum, *v.* 3 *a.*, to kill, destroy.

occŭpo, *v.* 1 *a.*, to seize.

occurro, -curri, -cursum, *v.* 3 *n.*, to meet.

octāvus, *adj.*, eighth.

ŏcŭlus, -i, *subs. m.*, eye.

ŏdium, -i, *subs. m.*, hatred.

off ro, obtuli, -latum, *v. irreg.*, to offer, present.

omitto, -misi, -missum, *v.* 3 *a.*, to let loose, let fall, abandon, give up.

omnis, -e, *adj.*, all.

ŏnustus, -e, *adj.*, laden.

ŏpem, -is, *subs. f.*, strength, help; *in pl.* resources, wealth.

ŏpĕra, -ae, *subs. f.*, pains, labour, service.

ŏpīmus, *adj.*, rich, fertile. *spolia —*, spoils taken from enemy's general.

ŏpīnio, -onis, *subs. f.*, opinion, expectation.

oppĭdanus, *adj.*, of a town, a townsman.

oppĭdum, -i, *subs. n.*, town.

opportūnus, *adj.*, convenient, seasonable, advantageous.

oppugnātio, -onis, *subs. f.*, assault, attack.

oppugno, *v.* 1 *a.*, to assault, attack.

ŏpŭlentus, *adj.*, wealthy.

ŏpus, -eris, *subs. n.*, work.

ŏrācŭlum, -i, *subs. n.*, oracle.

ŏrātor, -oris, *subs. m.*, speaker, ambassador, envoy.

orbis, -is, *subs. m.*, circle, round. — *terrae*, the world.

orbo, *v.* 1 *a.*, to bereave.

ordo, -inis, *subs. m.*, straight row, line, rank of soldiers; arrangement, order.

ŏrīgo, -inis, *subs. f.*, beginning, origin, race.

ŏrior, ortus, *v.* 4 *dep.*, to arise, begin.

ornātus, -ūs, *subs. m.*, equipment, dress.

ōro, *v.* 1 *a.*, to beg, beseech.

ōs, oris, *subs. n.*, mouth, face.

ostendo, -di, -sum *and* -tum, *v.* 3 *a.*, to show, display.

ostento, *v.* 1 *a.*, to show.

ŏvo, *v.* 1 *n.*, to celebrate an ovation, or lesser triumph; to exult, rejoice.

pāciscor, pactus, *v.* 3 *dep.*, to bargain.

pactio, -onis, *subs. f.*, a bargain, contract.

paene, *adv.*, almost.

paenĭtet, -uit, *v.* 2 *n. and a.*, to repent, *usually impersonal*, to cause to feel sorrow; *paenitet me*, I repent.

pălam, *adv.*, openly.

Pălatium, -i, *subs. n.*, one of the seven hills of Rome.

pālor, *v.* 1 *dep.*, to wander about.

pălūdatus, *adj.*, wearing the general's cloak.

pando, pandi, pansum *and* passum, *v.* 3 *a.*, to open; *perf. part.*, passus, loosened, disordered (of hair).

pānis, -is, *subs. m.*, bread.

pār, păris, *adj.*, equal.

pāreo, -ui, *v.* 2 *n.*, to obey.

părens, *subs. c.*, parent.

părio, peperi, partus, *v.* 3 *a.*,
to give birth to.
păro, *v.* 1 *a.*, to prepare.
pars, partis, *subs. f.*, part.
partĭceps, -cipis, *subs.*, a
sharer.
partio, *v.* 4 *a.*, to share, dis-
tribute.
părum, *adv.*, too little.
părumper, *adv.*, for a short
time.
parvus, *adj.*, small.
pastor, -ōris, *subs. m.*, shepherd.
pătĕfācio, -feci, -factum, *v.* 3
a., to open.
păteo, *v.* 2 *n.*, to be open.
păter, -tris, *subs. m.*, father.
pătientia, -ae, *subs. f.*, pa-
tience.
pătior, passus, *v.* 3 *dep.*, to
suffer, bear, allow.
pătria, -ae, *subs. f.*, native
land, country.
pătricius, *adj.*, patrician.
paucĭtas, -atis, *subs. f.*, few-
ness, scarcity.
paucus, *adj.*, few.
păveo, pāvi, *v.* 2 *n.*, to be
dismayed.
păvĭdus, *adj.*, terrified, panic-
stricken.
păvor, -ōris, *subs. m.*, panic.
pax, pācis, *subs. f.*, peace.
pectus, -ōris, *subs. n.*, breast.
pĕcus, -ōris, *subs. n.*, cattle;
esp. sheep, flock.
pĕdes, -itis, *subs. m.*, a foot
soldier.
pĕdester, -tris, -tre, *adj.*, on
foot, foot-.
pello, pepuli, pulsum, *v.* 3 *a.*,
to drive, put to flight.

pĕnes, *prep. gov. acc.* in the
power of.
pĕnĕtro, *v.* 1 *a.*, to penetrate,
make one's way into.
pĕnūria, -ae, *subs. f.*, dearth,
scarcity.
pĕr, *prep. gov. acc.*, through,
over, by means of.
perăgro, *v.* 1 *a.*, to travel
through, traverse.
percello, -cŭli, -culsum, *v.* 3
a., beat down, overthrow.
percunctor, *v.* 1 *dep.*, to ask,
inquire.
percŭtio, -cussi, -cussum, *v.* 3
a., to strike.
perdūco, -duxi, -ctum, *v.* 3 *a.*,
to lead through, induce.
pĕrĕgrīnus, *adj.*, foreign.
pereo, -ivi *or* -ii, -itum, *v.* 4
n., to perish.
perfĕro, -tuli, -latum, *v. irreg.*,
to bear through, convey.
perfĭcio, -feci, -fectum, *v.* 3
a., to finish, perform.
perfŭgio, -fūgi, -fugitum, *v.* 3
n., to flee for refuge.
pergo, -perrexi, -ctum, *v.* 3.
a. and n., to go straight on,
continue, proceed.
pĕrīculum, -i, *subs. m.*, danger.
pĕrītus, *adj.*, skilful, *gov. gen.*
permissus, -us, *subs. m.*, leave,
permission.
permitto, -misi, -missum, *v.*
3 *a.*, to let go, let loose,
give up, surrender, allow.
permulceo, -si, -sum, *v.* 2 *a.*,
to stroke gently, soothe.
perpĕtro, *v.* 1 *a.*, to accomplish.

persĕquor, -secutus, *v.* 3 *dep.*,
to pursue, follow up.

pervĕho, -xi, -ctum, *v.* 3 *a.*,
to carry through, convey.

pervĕnio, -vēni, -ventum, *v.*
4 *n.*, **to** arrive.

pervinco, -vīci, -victum, *v.* 3.
a., to **conquer,** induce, pre-
vail **on.**

pestis, -is, *subs. f.*, plague,
destruction, disaster.

pĕto, -ivi, -itum, *v.* 3 *a.*, to
seek, go towards, demand,
beg.

plăceo, -ui, -itum, *v.* 2 *n.*, to
be pleasing, please.

plaustrum, -i, *subs. m.*, **wagon.**

plēbes, -is, *subs. f.*, common
people, plebeians.

plēnus, *adj.*, full.

plerusque, *adj.*, **a great part;**
pl. very many, most.

pollĭceor, -itus, *v.* 2 *a.*, to
promise.

poena, -ae, *subs. f.*, **penalty,**
punishment.

pondo, *adv.*, by weight; *as
indecl. subs.*, a pound.

pondus, -eris, *subs. n.*, weight.

pōno, posui, positum, *v.* 3
a., to place, pitch (a camp),
put down, lay aside.

pons, pontis, *subs. m.*, bridge.

pŏpŭlaris, -e, *adj.*, of the
people, popular.

pŏpŭlatio, -**onis,** *subs. f.*, **a**
laying waste, devastation.

pŏpŭlator, -oris, *subs. m.*,
plunderer.

pŏpŭlor, *v.* 1 *dep.*, **to lay**
waste.

pŏpŭlus, -**i,** *subs. m.*, people,
nation.

Porsĕna, -ae, *subs. m.*, a king
of Clusium in Etruria.

porta, -ae, *subs. f.*, gate,
door.

portendo, -**di,** -tum, *v.* 3 *a.*,
to foretell, portend.

porto, *v.* 1 *a.*, **to carry.**

posco, poposci, *v.* 3 *a.*, **to**
demand.

possĭdeo, -**sedi,** -sessum, *v.* 2
a., **to possess.**

possum, **potui,** *v.* *irreg.*, **to be**
able.

postea, *adv.*, afterwards.

postĕrus, *adj.*, coming after,
following; *in compar.* **after,**
later ; *superl.* postremus,
latest, last.

postquam, *conj.*, after.

postrēmo, *adv.*, lastly.

postŭlātum, -i, *subs. n.*, a
demand.

postŭlo, *v.* 1 *a.*, to demand.

pŏtestas, -atis, *subs. f.*, **power.**

pŏtior, *v.* 4 *dep.*, to **get pos-**
session of, gain.

pŏtius, *adv.*, rather, prefer-
ably.

praealtus, *adj.*, very high.

praebeo, *v.* 2 *a.*, to hold out,
offer, display.

praeceps, -cipitis, *adj.*, headlong, steep, precipitous.

praeco, -onis, *subs. m.*, a crier,
herald.

praeda, -**ae,** *subs. f.*, **prey,**
booty, plunder.

praedīco, -**xi,** -ctum, *v.* 3 *a.*,
to **foretell.**

praedo, -onis, *subs. m.*, robber.

praedor, *v.* 1 *dep.*, to plunder.

praefectus, -i, *subs. m.*, gover-
nor.

praeféro, -tŭli, -latum, *v. irreg.*, to carry before ; prefer.

praemūnio, *v.* 4 *a.*, to fortify in front.

praeruptus, *adj.*, steep, abrupt.

praesĭdium, -i, *subs. n.*, guard.

praesto, -stiti, -stĭtum, *v.* 1 *a*, to stand before, excel, fulfil, discharge.

praesum, -fui, *v. irreg.*, to be before, be in command of.

praeter, *prep. gov. acc.*, except, beyond, beside.

praetĕreo, -Ivi or -ii, -itum, *v.* 4 *a.*, to pass by.

praevălens, *part.*, very strong.

prātum, -i, *subs. n.*, meadow.

prĕcem, -is, *subs. f.*, no nom., prayer, entreaty.

prĕcor, *v.* 1 *dep.*, to pray, entreat.

prīmum, *adv.*, first.

prīmo, *adv.*, at first.

prīmus, *adj. superl.*, first.

princeps, -ipis, *adj. and subs.*, first, chief.

princĭpālis, -e, *adj.*, of a chief. The via principalis was the street across a camp. porta p. dextra, and p. p. sinistra were the gates at either end of it.

prior, *adj. compar.*, former, earlier.

prius, *adv.*, earlier, before.

priusquam, *conj.*, before.

pristĭnus, *adj.*, former, original.

prīvātus, *adj.*, private.

pro, *prep. gov. abl.*, before, in front of.

Prŏcas, *or* -a, an ancient king of Alba.

prŏcēdo, -cessi, -cessum, *v.* 3 *n.*, proceed, advance.

prŏcella, -ae, *subs. f.*, storm.

prŏcer, -eris, *subs. m.*, a chief, noble (*usually in plural*).

prŏclīvis, -e, *adj.*, sloping forward ; *neut. used as subs.*, a slope, descent.

prŏcul, *adv.*, at a distance, far.

prŏdeo, -Ivi or -ii, -itum, *v.* 4 *n.*, to go forth.

prŏdĭgium, -i, *subs. n.*, an omen, portent.

prŏdo, -didi, -ditum, *v.* 3 *a.*, to betray.

proelium, -i, *subs. n.*, battle.

prŏfecto, *adv.*, assuredly, certainly.

prŏfero, -tuli, -latum, *v. irreg.*, to bring forward, produce.

prŏficio, -feci, -fectum, *v.* 3 *a. and n.*, to gain ground, advance, accomplish.

prŏficiscor, -fectus, *v.* 3 *dep.*, to set out.

prŏfūgio, -fūgi, -fŭgĭtūm, *v.* 3 *n.*, to run away, take refuge.

prŏgrĕdior, -gressus, *v.* 3 *dep.*, to advance.

prŏhĭbeo, *v.* 2 *a.*, to keep off, prevent, hinder.

prŏlābor, -lapsus, *v.* 3 *dep.*, to fall forward.

prŏmitto, -misi, -missum, *v.* 3 *a.*, to promise.

prŏpe, *prep. gov. acc. and adv.*, near, nearly.

prŏpĕre, *adv.*, hastily.

prŏpinquus, *adj.*, neighbouring.

prŏpĭtius, *adj.*, favourable, kind, propitious.

propter, *prep. gov. acc.*, on account of.

prosēco, -ui, -tum, *v.* 1 *a.*, to cut off, cut away the parts of a victim to be sacrificed.

prōsĕquor, -secutus, *v.* 3 *dep.*, to follow, accompany, pursue.

prospĕre, *adv.*, favourably, fortunately.

prospĭcio, -spexi, -spectum, *v.* 3 *a. and n.*, to look forward, take care of.

proturbo, *v.* 1 *a.*, to drive forward, dislodge.

provĕho, -vexi. -vectum, *v.* 3 *a.*, to carry forward.

provŏco, *v.* 1 *a.*, to call forth, challenge.

provŏlo, *v.* 1 *a.*, to rush forward.

proxĭmus, *adj. superl.* (prope), nearest, next.

pūber, -eris, *adj.*, grown up.

publīce, *adv.*, in behalf of the state, at the public cost.

publĭcus, *adj.*, belong to the state, public, general.

pŭdor, -oris, *subs. m.*, shame, modesty, sense of honour.

puer, -i, *subs. m.*, a boy.

puerīlis, -e, *adj.*, boyish, youthful.

pugna, -ae, *subs. f.*, a battle.

pulcrĭtudo, -inis, *subs. f.*, beauty.

pulvis, -eris, *subs. m.*, dust.

Pȳthĭcus, *adj.*, of Delphi, the ancient name of which was Pytho.

quācunque, *adv.*, wherever.

quaero, quaesivi, -situm, *v.* 3 *a.*, to ask, seek.

quam, *adv.*, how.

quamquam, *conj.*, although.

quando, *interrog. adv.*, when?

quantum, *adv.*, as much, so much as, how much.

quantus, *adj.*, how great. *tantus ... quantus*, as great ... as.

quātrĭduum, -i, *subs. n.*, a space of four days.

quātuor, *adj. indecl.*, four.

-que, *conj.*, and.

quērēla, -ae, *subs. f.*, a complaint.

quĕror, questus, *v.* 3 *dep.*, to complain.

qui, *rel. pron.*, who, which.

quĭa, *conj.*, because.

quīdam, *pron. and adj.*, a certain, a certain one.

quĭdem, *adv.*, indeed, in truth. *ne quidem*, not even.

quĭes, -ētis, *subs. f.*, rest.

quīlĭbet, *pron.*, any one.

quĭn, *conj.*, that not, but that, *after a negative and gov. subjunctive.*

quinque, *num. adj. indecl.*, five.

Quĭrīnālis, *adj.*, of Quirinus, or Romulus.

quis, *pron. interrog.*, who? what?

quisnam, *pron. interrog.*, who, pray?

quisquam, *pron.*, any one; *used after a negative.*

quisque, *pron.*, each.

quo, *adv.*, whither, to which place.

quod, *conj.*, because.

quominus, *conj.*, by which the less; that not; *with subj. mood after verbs of hindering, it may often be translated* from.

quŏnĭam, *conj.*, because.

quoque, *c nj.*, also.

quum, *conj.*, when, since, as. *quum ... tum*, both ... and.

răpio, rapui, -ptum, *v.* 3 *a.*, to seize, snatch, carry off by force, hurry.

raptim, *adv.*, violently, hastily.

raptus, -ūs, *subs. m.*, a carrying off.

rārus, *adj.*, thin, far apart, scattered, scanty, few.

rătio, -onis, *subs. f.*, reasoning, reason.

rătus, *part.* (from *reor*), settled, established, valid.

Rea Silvia, mother of Romulus and Remus.

rĕcens, *adj.*, fresh, new.

rĕcenseo, -ui, -sum, *v.* 2 *a.*, to review.

rĕceptus, -ūs, *subs. m.*, retreat.

rĕcĭpio, -cepi, -ceptum, *v.* 3 *a.*, to take back, recover; *se r.*, to retreat, withdraw.

rectus, *adj.*, straight, correct.

rĕcŭpĕro, *v.* 1 *a.*, to get back, recover.

rĕcūso, *v.* 1 *a.*, to refuse.

reddo, -didi, -ditum, *v.* 3 *a.*, to give back, restore, render.

rĕdeo, -ivi or -ii, -itum, *v.* 4 *a.*, to go back, return.

rĕdĭmo, -emi, -emptum, *v.* 3 *a.*, to buy back, redeem.

rĕfello, -felli, *v.* 3 *a.*, to disprove, prove to be false.

rĕfĕro, -tuli, -latum, *v.* 3 *a.*, to carry back, bring back: repay; report, or put a question to the senate or people; refer.

rĕfŭgio, -fūgi, -fugitum, *v.* 3 *n.*, to flee back, shrink back.

Regillus, a lake in Latium.

rĕgio, -onis, *subs. f.*, district, region.

rĕgius, *adj.*, of a king, royal.

regno, *v.* 1 *a.*, to reign.

regnum, -i, *subs. m.*, kingly power, kingdom.

rĕgo, -rexi, -ctum, *v.* 3 *a.*, to rule.

rĕgredior, -gressus, *r.* 3 *dep.*, to return.

rĕgŭlus, -i, *subs. m.*, a little king, chieftain.

rējĭcio, -jeci, -jectum, *r.* 3 *a*, to throw back, cast off, drive back.

rĕlinquo, -liqui, -lictum, *r.* 3 *a.*, to leave.

Rĕmus, brother of Romulus.

rĕnītor, -nisus *or* -nixus, *r.* 3 *dep.*, to struggle against, withstand, remonstrate.

rĕnŏvo, *r.* 1 *a.*, to renew.

reor, rātus, *r.* 2 *dep.*, to think, consider.

rĕpente, *adv.*, suddenly.

rĕpentinus, *adj.*, sudden.

rĕpēto, -ivi, -itum, *v.* 3 *a.*, to seek again, return to.

rĕpleo, -evi, -etum, *v.* 2 *a.*, to fill up.

res, rei, *subs. f.*, a thing, matter, business.

rĕsisto, -stiti, -stitum, *v.* 3 *n.*, to resist, withstand.

respecto, *v.* 1 *a.* and *n.*, to look back, look back at.

respergo, -spersi, -sum, *v.* 3 *a.*, to besprinkle.

respĭcio, -spexi, -ctum, *v.* 3 *a.* and *n.*, to look back, look back at.

respiro, *v.* 1 *a.* and *n.*, to breathe out, breathe ; to recover breath.

respondeo, -di, -sum, *v.* 2 *a.* and *n.*, to answer.

responsum, -i, *subs. n.*, answer.

restĭtuo, -ui, -utum, *v.* 3 *a.*, to restore, renew.

rĕtardo, *v.* 1 *a.*, to delay, impede.

rĕtrăho, -xi, -ctum, *v.* 3 *a.*, to draw back, withdraw.

rĕtro, *adv.*, backwards.

rĕtundo, -tudi, -tusum, or -tunsum, *v.* 3 *a.*, beat back, restrain, check.

reus, -i, *subs. m.*, an accused person, prisoner, guilty person.

rĕvello, -velli, -vulsum, *v.* 3 *a.*, to tear off.

rex, regis, *subs. m.*, king.

rĭgo, *v.* 1 *a.*, to wet, moisten; to convey water.

rīpa, -ae, *subs. f.*, bank.

rītĕ, *adv.*, with due religious rites ; duly, properly.

rĭtus, -ūs, *subs. m.*, a religious ceremony. *ritu*, after the manner of.

rīvus, -i, *subs. m.*, a stream, brook.

rōbur, -oris, *subs. n.*, hardness, vigour, power ; the best part of anything ; as we say, 'the flower.'

rŏgo, *v.* 1 *a.*, to ask.

Rōma, -ae, Rome.

Rōmŭlus, -i, the founder of Rome.

Rōmānus, *adj.*, Roman.

rŭber, -bra, -brum, *adj.*, red.

rumpo, rupi, ruptum, *v.* 3 *a.*, to burst, break asunder, break down, destroy.

ruptor, -oris, *subs. m.*, breaker, violator.

rursus, *adv.*, again.

Săbīnus, *adj.*, Sabine, the name of a Latin tribe near Rome.

săcellum, -i, *subs. n.*, a sanctuary, chapel.

săcerdos, -otis, *subs. c.*, priest, priestess.

sacrĭfĭcium, -i, *subs. n.*, sacrifice.

saepe, *adv.*, often.

saepio, saepsi, saeptum, *v.* 4 *a.*, to fence in, inclose.

saltus, -us, *subs. m.*, a mountain-pass, forest glade.

sălūs, -utis, *subs. f.*, health, safety.

sălūto, *v.* 1 *a.*, to greet, salute.

sanguis, -inis, *subs. m.*, blood.

sarcĭna, -ae, *subs. f.*, bundle, baggage.

sătelles, -itis, *subs. m.*, an attendant, guard.

sătis, *adv.*, enough.

saucius, *adj.*, wounded.

saxum, *subs. n.*, stone.

Scaevŏla, -ae, *subs.*, the left-handed; cognomen given to C. Mucius.

scando, -di, -sum, *v.* 3 *a.*, to climb.

scĕlus, -eris, *subs. n.*, crime.

scindo, scĭdi, scissum, *v.* 3 *a.*, to tear, cleave.

scio, scivi, scitum, *v.* 3 *a.*, to know.

scĭpio, -onis, *subs. m.*, staff.

sciscĭtor, *v.* 1 *dep.*, to inquire.

scrība, -ae, *subs. m.*, secretary.

scūtum, i, *subs. n.*, shield.

se, *reflex. pron.*, -self, oneself.

sĕcundus, *adj.*, following, second, favourable.

sĕcus, *adv.*, otherwise.

sĕd, *conj.*, but.

sĕdeo, sessi, sessum, *v.* 2 *n.*, to sit.

sēgrĕgo, *v.* 1 *a.*, to separate.

sella. -ae, *subs. f.*, chair.

sēmĭrŭtus, *adj.*, half-ruined.

semper, *adv.*, always.

sĕnātus, -us, *subs. m.*, the senate.

sĕnesco, senui, *v.* 3 *n.*, to grow old, wane, decline.

sĕnex, senis, *adj. and subs.*, old, old man.

sēni. *adj. distr.*, six apiece.

sensus. -ūs, *subs. m.*, feeling.

sententia, -ae, *subs. f.*, opinion.

sentio, sensi, -sum, *v.* 2 *a.*, to feel, perceive.

sĕpulcrum, -i, *subs. n.*, tomb.

sĕquor, secutus, *v.* 3 *dep.*, to follow.

sermo, -onis, *subs. m.*, conversation.

servitium, -i, *subs. m.*, slavery : a slave.

servo, *v.* 1 *a.*, to preserve, save.

sex, *indecl. adj.*, six.

siccus, *adj.*, dry.

Sĭcĭlla, Sicily.

signĭfĭco, *v.* 1 *a.*, to express by signs, show, indicate.

signum, -i, *subs. n.*, sign ; military standard.

sĭlentium, -i, *subs. m.*, silence.

sĭmĭlis, -e, *adj.*, like.

sĭmul, *adv.*, at the same time. Sometimes = *simul atque, conj.*, as soon as.

sĭmŭlacrum, -i, *subs. n.*, image, likeness.

sĭmŭlo, *v.* 1 *a.*, to pretend that something is which is not, to assume, counterfeit.

sĭne, *prep. gov. abl.*, without.

singŭli, *distrib. adj.*, one apiece, separate, single.

sĭnister, *adj.*, on the left. *sinistra,* the left hand.

sĭno, sivi, situm, *v.* 3 *a.*, to let, suffer, allow.

sĭtio, -ivi *or* -ii, *v.* 4 *n.*, to be thirsty.

sŏcer, -eri, *subs. m.*, father-in-law.

sŏcĭetas, -atis, *subs. f.*, alliance.

sŏcius, -i, *subs. m.*, **ally, partner.**

sŏlemnis, -e, *adj.*, annual, solemn, usual.

sŏlĭtūdo, -ĭnis, *subs. f.*, loneliness, solitude.

sollĭcĭtus, *adj.*, anxious.

sŏlum, -i, *subs. n.*, soil.

sŏlus, *adj.*, alone.

solvo, -vi, -ŭtum, *v.* 3 *a.*, to loosen, untie, break up.

sors, -tis, *subs. f.*, chance, lot.

sospes, -ĭtis, *adj.*, safe.

spătĭum, -i, *subs. n.*, space, interval of time or space.

spēcĭes, -ei, *subs. f.*, appearance.

spectāculum, -i, *subs. n.*, a spectacle, sight.

specto, *v.* 1 *a.*, to look at.

sperno, sprevi, spretum, *v.* 3 *a.*, to despise.

spēro, *v.* 1 *a.*, to hope.

spes, -ei, *subs. f.*, hope.

spīculum, -i, *subs. n.*, a dart, arrow, javelin.

spŏlio, *v.* 1 *a.*, to strip, spoil, plunder.

sponte, *adv.*, of one's own accord.

stătĭo, -onis, *subs. f.*, a post, station, guard ; *in pl.*, sentinels.

stătua, -ae, *subs. f.*, statue.

stătuo, -i, -tum, *v.* 3 *a.* to set up, appoint, decide.

sterno, stravi, stratum, *v.* 3 *a.*, to spread out, strew ; throw down, overthrow.

stĭmŭlo, *v.* 1 *a.*, to rouse, urge on.

stīpendĭum, -i, *subs. n.*, pay.

stirpes, -is, *subs. f.*, stock, offspring, family.

strāges, -is, *subs. f.*, destruction, slaughter.

strĕpĭtus, -ûs, *subs. m.*, crashing noise, din, uproar.

stŭdĭum, -i, *subs. n.*, zeal, eagerness.

stŭpĕfacio, -feci, -factum, *v.* 3 *a.*, to benumb, stun, amaze.

subdo, -dĭdi, -dĭtum, *v.* 3 *a.*, to put under, apply, substitute.

sŭbeo, -ivi or -ii, -itum, *v.* 4 *n.*, to go under, come up, approach.

sŭbĭgo, -egi, -actum, *v.* 3 *a.*, to subdue.

sŭbĭto, *adv.*, suddenly.

sŭbĭtus, *adj.*, sudden.

sublĕvo, *v.* 1 *a.*, to lift up, support.

Sublĭcĭus pons, the oldest bridge of Rome.

sublustris, -e, *adj.*, dim, having faint light.

submŏveo, -mōvi, -motum, *v.* 2 *a.*, to remove, dislodge, clear away.

subruo, -rŭi, -rŭtum, *v.* 3 *a.*, to undermine.

subsĕquor, -secutus, *v.* 3 *dep.*, to follow closely.

subsĭdiarius, *adj.*, *in pl.* as *subs.*, reserves.

subsĭdium, -i, *subs. n.*, the reserve, reinforcement, support.

succēdo, -cessi, -cessum, *v.* 3 *a.*, to mount, ascend, approach, to come into the place of.

successus, -us, *subs. m.,* success.

sūdor, -oris, *subs. m.,* sweat.

sum, fui, *v. irreg.,* to be.

sūmo, sumpsi, sumptum, *v.* 3 *a.,* to take up.

sumptus, -ūs, *subs. m.,* expense.

sŭper, *prep. gov. acc. and abl.,* above, over, in addition to.

sŭperbia, -ae, *subs. f.,* pride, haughtiness.

sŭperbus, *adj.,* haughty.

sŭperincĭdo, *v.* 3, to fall on the top of.

sŭpěro, *v.* 1 *a.,* to overcome.

sŭpersum, -fui, *v. irreg.,* to be over, to survive.

sŭpěrus, *adj.,* high above.

supplex, -icis, *adj.,* suppliant, submissive.

supplicātĭo, -onis, *subs. f.,* thanksgiving.

supplĭcium, -i, *subs. n.,* punishment, execution.

sŭper, *adv. and prep. gov. acc.,* above.

suspĭcor, *v.* 1 *dep.,* to suspect.

sustĭneo, -ui, -tentum, *v.* 2 *a.,* to sustain, uphold, support.

suus, *poss. pron. and adj.,* one's own.

tăberna, -ae, *subs. f.,* shop.

taedium, -i, *subs. n.,* weariness, disgust.

tămen, *conj.,* nevertheless, however.

tandem, *adv.,* at length.

tango, tetigi, tactum, *v.* 3 *a.,* to touch.

tantum, *adv.,* only.

tantus, *adj.,* so great.

Tarquĭnius, the name of the last royal family at Rome.

tectum, -i, *subs. n.,* roof, house.

tēgŭla, -ae, *subs. f.,* tile.

tēlum, -i, *subs. n.,* dart, weapon.

tĕmĕre, *adv.,* rashly, at random.

templum, -i, *subs. n.,* temple.

tempus, -oris, *subs. n.,* time.

tĕneo, -ui, -tentum, *v.* 2 *a.,* to hold.

tergum, -i, *subs. n.,* back.

terni, *adj. distr.,* three each.

terreo, *v.* 2 *a.,* to frighten.

terror, -oris, *subs. m.,* fear, terror.

tertius, *adj.,* third.

testūdo, -inis, *subs. f.,* tortoise (see note).

Tĭbĕris, -is, *subs. m.,* the Tiber.

Tĭbĕrīnus, *adj.,* of the Tiber; *pater Tiberinus,* 'father Tiber.'

tĭmeo, -ui, *v.* 2 *a.,* to fear.

tĭmor, -oris, *subs. m.,* fear.

tŏga, -ae, *subs. f.,* toga, the robe worn by Romans.

tŏgatus, *adj.,* wearing the toga.

tollo, sustuli, sublatum, to lift, take away, carry off.

tōtus, *adj.,* whole.

trādo, -didi, -ditum, *v.* 3 *a.,* to hand over, give up; hand down, record.

trăho, -xi, -ctum, *v.* 3 *a.,* to draw, drag, prolong.

trājĭcio, -jeci, -jectum, *v.* 3 *a.*
and *n.*, to throw across,
transport, cross.

trāno, *v.* 1 *a.*, to swim across.

transeo, -ivi *or* -ii, -itum, *v.* 4
a., to cross.

transfĕro, -tuli, -latum, *v.* 3 *a.*,
to carry **over,** remove,
transfer.

transfīgo, -fixi, -fixum, *v.* 3 *a.*,
to pierce through.

transfŭga, -ae, *subs. m.*, a
deserter.

transgrĕdior, -gressus, *v.* 3
dep., to cover over.

transĭgo, -egi, -actum, *v.* 3 *a.*,
to finish, settle, transact.

transĭlio, -ui, *v.* 4 *a.*, to leap
across.

transvĕho, -vexi, -vectum, *v.*
3 *a.*, to carry across.

transversus, *adj.*, crosswise :
ex *transverso*, sideways.

trĕcenti, *adj.*, three hundred.

trĕpĭdatio, **-onis,** *subs. f.*,
trembling, alarm.

trĕpĭdo, *v.* 1 *a.*, to tremble,
be alarmed.

trĕpĭdus, *adj.*, trembling,
alarmed.

tres, tria, *adj.*, three.

triārii, *subs. m. pl.*, the vete-
ran soldiers, who formed
the third line ; the reserve.

trĭbūnal, -alis, *subs. n.*, plat-
form, judgment seat.

trĭbūnĭcius, *adv.*, of the tribunes.

trĭbūnus, -i, *subs. m.*, a tribune. 1. — *plebis*, tribune of
the people, whose duty it
was to defend the plebeians
against the patrician mag-

istrates. **2.** — *militum consulari potestate* were appointed instead of consuls
from A.D. 444-366. They
were **at** first three, then
six, then eight in number.
3. — *militum*, tribunes **of**
the soldiers ; officers of the
army, of whom there were
six to **each** legion.

trĭbūtum, -i, *subs. n.*, tribute,
tax.

trĭennĭum, -i, *subs. n.*, a space
of three years.

trĭgĕmĭni, -orum, three twin
brothers.

triumphālis, **-e.** *adj.*, **of** a
triumph, triumphal.

triumpho, *v.* 1 *a.*, to celebrate a triumph.

triumphus, -i, *subs. m.*, **a**
triumph. The solemn en-
trance of a general into
Rome after **a** great victory.

trux, trucis, *adj.*, fierce,
stern, threatening.

tueor, tuitus, *v.* 2 *dep.*, **to**
gaze at, protect.

tŭgŭrium, **-i,** *subs. m.*, **hut,**
cottage.

Tullius, Attius, **a** Volscian
chief **who** received Coriolanus.

Tullus Hostilius, one of the
seven kings of Rome.

tum, *adv.*, then.

tŭmultus, -us, *subs. m.*, uproar, insurrection, civil war.

turba, -ae, *subs. f.*, a crowd.

turbo, *v.* 1 *a.*, to throw into
confusion.

turma, -ae, *subs. f.*, a troop
of horse; troop.

Tuscŭlānus, *adj.*, of Tusculum.

Tuscus, *adj.*, Etruscan.

tūtor, *v.* 1 *dep.*, to guard,
protect.

tūtus, *adj.*, safe.

tўrannus, -i, *subs. m.*, a de-
spotic ruler, tyrant.

ŭbi, *adv.*, where.

ullus, *adj.*, any.

ultor, -oris, *subs. m.*, avenger.

ultĭmus, *adj. superl.*, last
(*from ultra*).

ultra, *adv. and prep. gov.
acc.*, beyond.

ŭlŭlatus, -us, *subs. m.*, howl-
ing, wailing.

umbo, -onis, *subs. m.*, the boss
projecting from the centre
of a shield.

undĕcĭmus, *adj.*, eleventh.

undĭque, *adv.*, from all
sides.

ūnĭcus, *adj.*, only.

ūnus, *adj.*, one.

urbs, urbis, *subs. f.*, city.

urgeo. ursi. *v.* 2 *a. and n.*,
to press, press hard on.

usquam, *adv.*, anywhere.

ŭt, *adv. and conj.*: (1) *with
indic.*, how, when, as; (2)
with subj., that, so that, in
order that.

ŭter, -tra, -trum, *adj.*, which
of two.

ŭterque, each of two.

ŭtĭque, *adv.*, anyhow, in any
case.

ŭtor, usus, *v.* 3 *dep., gov. abl.*,
to use.

utpŏte, *adv.*, inasmuch as,
since.

ŭtrimque, *adv.*, on each side.

uxor, -oris, *subs. f.*, wife.

vacuus, *adj.*, empty, free
from.

vādo, vasi, vasum, *v.* 3 *a.*, to
go.

vae, *interj.*, alas! woe!

vāgītus, -ūs, *subs. m.*, wailing.

văgor, *v.* 1 *dep.*, to wander.

văgus, *adj.*, wandering.

văleo, -ui, *v.* 2 *n.*, to be well,
be strong.

vălĭdus, *adj.*, strong.

vallum, -i, *subs. n.*, rampart.

vallus, -i, *subs. m.*, a wooden
stake.

vānus, *adj.*, vain, useless,
false.

vastus, *adj.*, empty, deserted,
vast, immense.

vātes, -is, *subs. m.*, a prophet.

vĕhĭcŭlum, -i, *subs. m.*, a
carriage.

Veiens, -entis, *adj.*, of
Veii.

Veii, -orum, *subs. m. pl.*, a
town of Etruria, taken by
Camillus.

vēlo, *v.* 1 *a.*, to cover, veil.

vĕlut, *adv.*, just as, like.

vĕnĕrābundus, *adj.*, full of
reverence, reverential.

vĕnio, vēni, ventum, *v.* 3 *n.*,
to come.

vēnor, *v.* 1 *dep.*, to hunt.

vĕreor, veritus, *v.* 2 *dep.*, to
fear.

versus, *prep. gov. acc.*, towards.

vertex, -icis, *subs. m.*, eddy, whirlpool; top, highest point.

verto, ti, -sum, *v.* 3 *a* and *n.*, to turn, change.

vĕrus, *adj.*, true, real.

Vesta, -ae, the goddess of the hearth-fire and home.

Vestālis, *adj.*, of Vesta. *virgo vestalis*, vestal virgin, a priestess of Vesta.

vestĭbŭlum, -i, *subs. n.*, the entrance to a house.

vestīgium, -i, *subs. n.*, footprint.

vestis, -is, *subs. f.*, garment, dress.

vĕto, -ui, -itum, *v.* 1 *a.*, to forbid.

vĕtus, -eris, *adj.*, old, ancient.

vĕtustus, *adj.*, old, antique.

vĭa, -ae, *subs. f.*, way, road.

vīcīnus, *adj.*, neighbouring.

victĭma, -ae, *subs. f.*, victim, beast for sacrifice.

victor, -oris, *subs. m.*, conqueror.

victōria, -ae, *subs. f.*, victory.

vĭdeo, vidi, visum, *v.* 2 *a.*, to see.

vĭgĭlo, *v.* 1 *a.*, to watch, be awake.

vincio, vinxi, -netum, *v.* 4 *a.*, to bind.

vinco, vici, victum, *v.* 3 *a.*, to conquer.

vincŭlum, -i, *subs. m.*, a bond, chain.

vindĭco, *v.* 1 *a.*, to claim, avenge.

vīnum, -i, *subs. m.*, wine.

vĭŏlātor, -oris, *subs. m.*, violator.

vĭŏlo, *v.* 1 *a.*, to violate, break (one's word, a treaty, etc.)

vĭr, -i, *subs. m.*, a man, a husband.

virgo, -inis, *subs. f.*, a virgin, maiden.

virtus, -utis, *subs. f.*, manliness, valour.

vis, *subs. f.*, violence, force; *pl.*, *vires*, -ium, strength.

vīvo, vixi, victum, *v.* 3 *n.*, to live.

vix, *adv.*, scarcely.

vŏco, *v.* 1 *a.*, to call.

vŏlĭto, *v.* 1 *a.*, to fly to and fro, hover.

vŏlo, *v.* 1 *a.*, to fly.

vŏlo, velle, vŏlui, *v. irreg.*, to wish.

Volscus, a Volscian, one of the tribes of Latium.

vŏlŭcris, -is, *subs. f.*, a bird.

vŏluptas, -atis, *subs. f.*, pleasure.

vox, vōcis, *subs. f.*, voice.

vulgo, *v.* 1 *a.*, to make generally known, spread abroad, publish.

vulnĕro, *v.* 1 *a.*, to wound.

vulnus, -eris, *subs. n.*, a wound.

ENGLISH INDEX.

For information about the Latin words, refer to the Vocabulary.

A

add, to, *adjicio.*
against, *contra, in.*
age, *aetas.*
aid, *auxilium.*
ally, *socius.*
although, *etsi.*
amaze, *obstupefacio.*
ambassador, *legatus.*
ambush, *insidiae.*
announce, *nuntio.*
answer, to, *respondeo.*
answer, an, *responsum.*
anyone, *quisquam.*
appoint, *creo.*
approach, *adeo, advenio.*
approve of, *approbo.*
arise, *orior.*
armed, *armatus.*
arms, *arma.*
army, *exercitus.*
arouse, *excito.*
arrange, *constituo.*
arrival, *adventus.*
as, *ut, quum.*

ask, *rogo.*
ask for, *peto.*
attack, *aggredior, adorior.*
attempt, *conor.*

B

bank, *ripa.*
bargaining, *pactio.*
battle, *pugna, proelium.*
be present, *adsum.*
bear, *fero.*
before (*prep.*), *ante.*
before (*adv.*), *antea.*
beg, *oro.*
beg for, *peto.*
begin, *incipio, ineo.*
believe, *credo.*
besiege, *obsideo.*
between, *inter.*
body, *corpus.*
booty, *praeda.*
boy, *puer.*
brilliant, *clarus.*
brave, *fortis.*
break down, *interrumpo.*

break into, *irrumpo.*
bring, *affero.*
bring up, *educo.*
bridge, *pons.*
brother, *frater.*
build, *aedifico.*
building, *aedificium.*
but, *sed, autem.*
by, *a, ab.*

C

cackling, *clangor.*
call, *voco, appello.*
camp, *castra.*
can, *possum.*
Capitol, *Capitolium.*
carry, *fero.*
carry in, *infero.*
carry down, *defero.*
carry **off,** *aufero.*
carry on, *gero.*
cattle, *pecus.*
cause, *causa.*
cavalry, *equitatus.*
centre, *medius (adj.).*
certain, a, *quidam.*
chair, *sella.*
challenge, *provoco.*
chance, *occasio.*
change, *muto.*
chariot, *currus.*
chiefly, *maxime.*
chieftain, *regulus.*
child, *infans, puer.*
choose, *lego, deligo.*
citadel, *arx.*
citizen, *civis.*
city, *urbs.*
clan, *gens.*
climb, *scando, ascendo.*
collect, *confero, cogo.*
come, *venio.*

command, *jubeo, impero.*
companion, *comes.*
compel, *cogo.*
confer, *defero.*
conquer, *vinco.*
conspire, *conjuro.*
consul, *consul.*
consult, *consulo.*
conversation, *sermo.*
corn, *frumentum.*
country, *ager, rus.*
courage, *virtus.*
cross, *transeo,* **trajicio.**
crowd, *turba.*
cry, *clamor.*

D

danger, *periculum.*
daring, *audacia.*
day-break, *prima lux.*
decided, it is, *placet.*
defend, *defendo.*
demand, *postulo.*
descend, *descendo.*
desert, *desero.*
design, *consilium.*
desire, *cupido.*
determine, *constituo.*
dig, *fodio.*
disaster, *clades.*
discordant, *dissonus.*
distance, *spatium.*
distance, **at a,** *procul.*

E

each, *uterque.*
each side, on, *utrimque.*
eagerness, *ardor.*
easy, *facilis.*
eleventh, *undecimus.*
engage (in battle), *consero.*

enrol, *conscribo*.
enter, *ingredior*.
entice, *elicio*.
entrails, *exta*.
entrance (to a house), *vestibulum*.
entrenchment, *vallum*.
escape, *effugio*.
exclaim, *clamo*.
exile, *exilium*.
explain, *expono*.

F

father, *pater*.
fault, *culpa*.
fear (*verb*), *timeo*, *vereor*.
fear (*subs.*), *timor*.
few, *paucus*.
field, *ager*, *campus*.
fierce, *atrox*.
fight, to, *pugno*.
fight, a, *pugna*.
fill, *compleo*, *impleo*.
find, *invenio*.
first, *primus*.
flee, *fugio*.
foe, *hostes*.
follow, *sequor*.
following, *adj.*, *posterus*.
force, *vis*.
a force of men, *manus*.
forebode, *portendo*.
former, *pristinus*.
fortify, *munio*.
from, *a*, *ab*.
from all sides, *undique*.
found, to, *condo*.

G

gain, *adipiscor*.
game, *ludus*.
gather, *colligo*.

general, *imperator*.
give, *do*.
,, back, *reddo*.
,, up, *dedo*.
glory, *gloria*.
go, *eo*.
,, away, *abeo*.
,, out, *exeo*.
gold, *aurum*.
goose, *anser*.
grandson, *nepos*.
grateful, *gratus*.
guard, *custos*.

H

hand, to be at, *adsum*.
hand over, *trado*.
hand to hand, *cominus*.
hastily, *propere*.
have, *habeo*.
headlong, *praeceps*.
hear, *audio*.
height, *altitudo*.
help (*subs.*), *auxilium*.
help, to, *juvo*.
hill, *collis*.
himself, *se : ipse*.
hold, *teneo*.
,, (contain), *capio*.
,, at bay, *sustineo*.
hope (*subs.*), *spes*.
,, to, *spero*.
horseman, *eques*.
hunger, *fames*.
hurl, *jacio*, *conjicio*.
hurl down, *dejicio*.

I

increase, to (*intrans.*), *cresco*.
infantry, *peditatus*, *pedites* (*pl.*)

people, *populus.*
  ,,   common, *plebs.*
perform, *fungor, defungor.*
perish, *pereo.*
place, *locus.*
plan, *consilium.*
plunder, *praeda.*
portent, *prodigium.*
position, *locus.*
pound, *pondo.*
prayer, *precem.*
prepare, *paro.*
present, to be, *adsum.*
in presence of, *coram.*
press, *urgeo.*
price, *pretium.*
priest, *sacerdos.*
proclaim, *edico.*
prolong, *produco.*
promise, *promitto, polliceor.*
prophet, *vates.*
pull, *traho.*
pursue, *sequor, insequor.*
put (under), *subdo.*

R

raid, *incursio.*
reach, *pervenio ad.*
reason, *causa.*
receive, *accipio, excipio.*
recognise, *agnosco.*
refer, *refero.*
renew, *renovo.*
repent, *poenitet.*
reply, *respondeo.*
reserves, *subsidiarii*
restore, *reddo.*
return, to, *redeo.*
return (*subs.*), *reditus.*
revolt, to, *deficere.*
right, *jus.*

right hand, *dextra.*
rise, *surgo.*
river, *flumen.*
robber, *latro.*
rock, *saxum.*
room, *spatium.*
rouse, *excito, concito.*
rout, to, *fundo.*
royal power, *regnum.*
rule, *rego.*
run off, *discurro.*
rush (*subs.*), *impetus.*

S

save, *servo.*
say, *dico.*
scarcity, *penuria.*
scorn, to, *sperno.*
second, *secundus, alter.*
see, *video.*
seek, *peto.*
seem, *videor.*
seize, *rapio, occupo.*
sell, *vendo.*
senate, *senatus.*
senator, *senator.*
send, *mitto.*
send away, *dimitto.*
sentry, *custos.*
separate (*intrans.*), *discurro.*
set fire to, *injicio.*
set out, *proficiscor.*
shame, *pudor.*
shepherd, *pastor.*
shop, *taberna.*
shout, *clamo.*
show, *monstro.*
shut, *claudo.*
shut in, *includo.*
siege, *obsidio.*
signal, *signum.*

sit, **sedeo.**
six, *sex.*
skilled, *peritus.*
slay, *interficio.*
sleep, *dormio.*
some ... others, *alii ... alii.*
son, *filius.*
soon, *mox.*
soothsayer, **haruspex.**
spear, *hasta.*
spectacle, *spectaculum.*
speed, *celeritas.*
spoil, *spolio.*
spur, calcar.
staff, *scipio.*
statue, *statua.*
steel, *ferrum.*
story, *fabula.*
stream, *flumen.*
stretch out, *extendo.*
strike, *percutio.*
strong, *firmus, validus.*
suitable, *aptus, idoneus.*
summon, *arcesso.*
surname, *cognomen.*
surround, *cingo.*
survive, *supersum.*
swim across, trano.

T

take, *capio.*
  ,, away, *aufero.*
  ,, up, *sumo.*
tear off, *detraho.*
territory, *fines.*
thanks, *grates, gratiae.*
think, *reor.*
this, *hic.*
thousand, *mille.*
three, *tres.*
three hundred, *trecenti.*

throw down, *dejicio.*
town, *oppidum.*
townsman, *oppidanus.*
treat (for peace, etc.), *ago.*
treaty, *foedus.*
truce, *indutiae.*
turn, verto.
twin, geminus.
two, two.

U

uncertain, *incertus.*
unharmed, *incolumis,* in-
unhurt, *teger, inviolatus.*
unless, *nisi.*
unite, *jungo.*
unprotected, *intutus.*
until, *donec.*

V

victim, hostia, *victima*
victory, victoria.

W

wage, **gero.**
wailing, *vagitus.*
wear, *bellum.*
wear **out,** *conficio.*
weight, *pondus.*
well **known,** it is, *constat.*
when, *quum, ubi.*
whether, *utrum.*
which (of two), *uter.*
who { (rel.), *qui.*
     { (interrog.), *quis.*
whole, *totus.*

wife, *conjux, uxor.*
will (*subs.*), *voluntas.*
win back, *redimo.*
winter-quarters, *hibernacula.*
wish, *volo.*
with, *cum.*
withstand, *resisto, sustineo.*
woe ! *vae.*
woman, *mulier.*

wound, a, *vulnus.*
wound, to, *vulnero.*

Y

yoke, *jugum.*
young, *juvenis.*
youth, a, *juvenis.*
youth, *juventus.*

PRINTED BY ROBERT MACLEHOSE, AT THE UNIVERSITY PRESS, GLASGOW.

MACMILLAN'S ELEMENTARY CLASSICS.

18mo, Eighteenpence each.

The following Elementary Books, with Introductions, Notes, and Vocabularies, and in some cases with Exercises, are either ready or in preparation:—

Aeschylus.—PROMETHEUS VINCTUS. Edited by Rev. H. M. STEPHENSON, M.A.

Caesar.—THE GALLIC WAR. Book I. Edited by A. S. WALPOLE, M.A.

THE INVASION OF BRITAIN. Being Selections from Books IV. and V. of the "De Bello Gallico." Adapted for the use of Beginners. With Notes, Vocabulary, and Exercises, by W. WELCH, M.A., and C. G. DUFFIELD, M.A.

THE GALLIC WAR. Books II. and III. Edited by the Rev. W. G. RUTHERFORD, M.A., LL.D.

THE GALLIC WAR. Book IV. Edited by C. BRYANS, M.A., Assistant Master at Dulwich College.

THE GALLIC WAR. Book V. Edited by C. COLBECK, M.A., Assistant Master at Harrow.

THE GALLIC WAR. Scenes from Books V. and VI. Edited by C. COLBECK, M.A., Assistant Master at Harrow.

Cicero.—DE SENECTUTE. Edited by E. S. SHUCKBURGH, M.A., late Fellow of Emanuel College, Cambridge.

DE AMICITIA. By the same Editor.

STORIES OF ROMAN HISTORY. Adapted for the use of Beginners. With Notes, Vocabulary, and Exercises by the Rev. G. E. JEANS, M.A., and A. V. JONES, M.A., Assistant Masters at Haileybury College.

Eutropius.—Adapted for the use of Beginners. With Notes, Vocabulary, and Exercises, by WILLIAM WELCH, M.A., and C. G. DUFFIELD, M.A.

Homer.—ILIAD. Book I. Edited by Rev. JOHN BOND, M.A., and A. S. WALPOLE, M.A.

ILIAD. Book XVIII. THE ARMS OF ACHILLES. Edited by S. R. JAMES, M.A., Assistant Master at Eton College.

ODYSSEY. Book I. Edited by Rev. JOHN BOND, M.A., and A. S. WALPOLE, M.A.

Horace.—ODES. Books I.—IV. Edited by T. E. PAGE, M.A., Cambridge; Assistant Master at the Charterhouse. Each 1s. 6d.

Livy.—Book I. Edited by H. M. STEPHENSON, M.A.

THE HANNIBALIAN WAR. Being part of the XXI. and XXII. Books of Livy, adapted for the use of Beginners, by G. C. MACAULAY, M.A.

THE SIEGE OF SYRACUSE. Being part of the XXIV. and XXV. Books of Livy, adapted for the use of Beginners. With Notes, Vocabulary, and Exercises, by GEORGE RICHARDS, M.A., and A. S. WALPOLE, M.A.

Lucian,—EXTRACTS FROM LUCIAN. Edited with Notes, Exercises, and Vocabulary, by Rev. JOHN BOND, M.A., and A. S. Walpole, M.A.

Cornelius Nepos.—SELECTIONS ILLUSTRATIVE OF GREEK AND ROMAN HISTORY. Edited for the use of Beginners, with Exercises by G. S. FARNELL, M.A., Assistant Master in St. Paul's School.

Ovid.—SELECTIONS. Edited by E. S. SHUCKBURGH, M.A.

Phaedrus.—SELECT FABLES. Adapted for the use of Beginners, with Notes, Exercises, and Vocabularies, by A. S. WALPOLE, M.A.

Thucydides.—THE RISE OF THE ATHENIAN EMPIRE. BOOK I., cc. LXXXIX.-CXVII. and CXXVIII.-CXXXVIII. Edited with Notes, Vocabulary, and Exercises by F. H. COLSON, M.A.

Virgil.—ÆNEID. BOOK I. Edited by A. S. WALPOLE, M.A.
ÆNEID. BOOK V. Edited by Rev. A. CALVERT, M.A.
SELECTIONS. Edited by E. S. SHUCKBURGH, M.A.

Xenophon.—ANABASIS. BOOK I. Edited by A. S. WALPOLE, M.A.
SELECTIONS FROM THE CYROPÆDIA. Edited with Notes, Vocabulary, and Exercises, by A. H. COOKE, M.A.

The following more advanced Books, with Introductions and Notes, **but no Vocabulary,** are either ready or in preparation :—

Cicero.—SELECT LETTERS. Edited by Rev. G. E. JEANS, M.A.

Euripides.—HECUBA. Edited by Rev. JOHN BOND, M.A., and A. S. WALPOLE, M.A.

Herodotus.—SELECTIONS FROM BOOKS VI. AND VII. THE EXPEDITION OF XERXES. Edited by A. H. COOKE, M.A.

Horace.—SELECTIONS FROM THE SATIRES AND EPISTLES. Edited by Rev. W. J. V. BAKER, M.A.
SELECT EPODES AND ARS POETICA. Edited by H. A. DALTON, M.A.

Plato.—EUTHYPHRO AND MENEXENUS. Edited by C. E. GRAVES, M.A.

Terence.—SCENES FROM THE ANDRIA. Edited by F. W. CORNISH, M.A.

The Greek Elegiac Poets.—FROM CALLINUS TO CALLIMACHUS. Selected and Edited by Rev. HERBERT KYNASTON, D.D., Principal of Cheltenham College.

Thucydides. BOOK IV. CHS. I.—XLI. THE CAPTURE OF SPHACTERIA. Edited by C. E. GRAVES, M.A.

Virgil.—GEORGICS. BOOK II. Edited by Rev. J. H. SKRINE, M.A.

*** *Other Volumes to follow.*